"Kick, Mule!"

by

John B Holway

Zeta Publishing

Ocala, FL

Zeta Publishing, Inc
3850 SE 58th Ave
Ocala, FL 34480
www.zetapublishing.com

Ordering Information:
Quantity sales. Special discounts are available on quantity purchases by corporations, associations, and others. For details, contact the publisher at the address above.
Orders by U.S. trade bookstores and wholesalers. Please contact Zeta Publishing: Tel: (352) 694-2553; Fax: (352) 694-1791 or visit www.zetapublishing.com

First published by Aeon Publishing in 2009

Rev. Date: 9/2017

ISBN: 978-1-947191-40-2 (sc)

ISBN: 978-1-947191-92-1 (e)

Library of Congress Control Number: 2017956378

Printed in the United States of America

To Eileen

PREFACE

This book has been 25 years in the making, the result of research into thousands of box scores and interviews with 76 veterans, covering a century of history.

Mule Samson was not a real person, though Mule Suttles was, and fans really did shout, "Kick, Mule" when he came to bat. Like most of the other men and women in the story, he is many men, who help fans of today travel on a voyage to yesterday. Mule is part Mule Suttles (who really was a coal-miner and a great slugger) and part Josh Gibson (who really was a shy youngster, later a suspected drug addict, and baseball's greatest slugger).

The adventures that happened to them actually did happen to real-life veterans of the Negro Leagues. I hope they will help readers today know and understand the great men of the black leagues and the world they lived in and overcame.

These pages are dedicated to Mule, Josh, Cool, Satch, Jud, Buck, Doc, Skinny, Duty, and all those who fought and won the battle to tear down the hurdles, and to Wilkie, Dizzy, Heath, and others who helped them do it.

I acknowledge a great debt to "Fredrico" Brillhart, Joe DeFazio, Dolly Patella, and Rob Langenderfer for their perceptive editing, which greatly improved what you read below.

John B Holway

“KICK, MULE!”

PROLOGUE

1973

COOPERSTOWN HALL OF FAME

A hot summer afternoon. The sound track plays *Thanks for the Memory* as a crowd moves slowly past the well-known Museum façade and onto the lawn beyond. The hillside is already filled with fans. On a dais beside the building, a row of empty folding chairs faces the crowd. In front of the dais, guests of honor are seated, including four black men in their 70s.

Buck's hair is white, but he is still as trim as he was in his playing days. He smiles the smile of a man who has criss-crossed the country for thirty years. He has seen it all, understands it all, and accepts it all.

"Skinny" is light-skinned, nervous, and too short to look over the lady's hat in front of him. He appears still as nimble as when he hopped after ground balls at shortstop. He smiles the mischievous smile of the clown and prankster, who kept the clubhouse loose with his practical jokes.

Double Duty - he could both pitch and catch - is a cherubic Chinese god of good fortune who led the league in most girl friends per season for nine years in a row. He surveys the crowd, checking out the best-looking women. His eye lights on one, and he gives her a cheerful smile, a nod, and a salute with gnarled and knotty fingers, which have been broken many times catching foul tips and blocking mammoth runners trying to score.

Skinny — short and balding, was one of best spit-ball pitchers in America - "Satchel Paige with his legs cut off."

Next to them sit Clara, a diminutive, gray-haired lady of the same age, and her daughter, Effie.

The baseball commissioner steps to the microphone.

"Ladies and gentlemen - the members of the Hall of Fame!"

As he reads each name, the player enters, waving to the cheers.

"Hank Aaron... Ernie Banks... Yogi Berra... Dizzy Dean... Roy Campanella.... Joe DiMaggio ... Bobby Feller... Lefty Grove... Stan Musial ... Satchel Paige... Tom Seaver ... Warren Spahn... Casey Stengel... Ted Williams.

"And the newest members of the Hall of Fame - Mickey Mantle... Sandy Koufax... Willie Mayberry..." - loud whistles and clapping from the crowd - "Cool Papa Bell... Mule Samson!"

Buck reaches for Clara's hand while Effie squeezes the other. Clara bites her lip and smiles softly. Buck leans over to Duty.

"Did you ever think we'd see this day, Duty?"

"No, Buck, I sure never did."

"Were you worried it would rain?"

"Nah, I don't worry about anything any more. I already did all my worryin' in the Negro Leagues."

PART I

1930

TOTAL DARK

Clanking and voices are heard and grow louder. Soon lights appear around a corner in a tunnel. They are flashlights and headlamps of black miners tramping to work. In their midst a mule pulls an iron coal cart along a track; it suddenly stops and gives the cart a sharp kick with a clang that echoes through the tunnel. The cart tumbles sideways onto one of the men.

Cussing. Shouts.

Several miners tug, trying to pull the man out. One miner, no more than 17 years old, turns quickly and runs to help. He puts his shoulder to the cart and strains. Grunting, he tries again. The cart slowly rises, and the victim is pulled free.

The miners crowd around. Their lamps light the face of the rescuer. It's a young face, a round face, streaming with sweat from the exertion.

"Heh, it's the kid!"

"That ain't no kid. It's a *mule*! How the hell did he do that?"

"Don't you know? That's his brother."

A DUSTY ROAD

Two figures, one on crutches, trudge uphill and stop to rest on a roadside rock to let a "tin lizzie" auto chug and rattle past. It kicks up dust and gravel, and they shield their faces, then watch it disappear over the hill below some clouds. "Somewhere, Over the Rainbow," plays quietly.

The younger man spits. "Man," he says. "I wish I had a car. I'd drive out of that damn mine and never come back."

"Where would you go?" his brother, Charlie, asks.

"Chicago," the kid says wistfully... "New York... California." He closes his eyes.

They sit quietly, wrapped in thought. Then they stand and turn back down toward the rough miners' shacks below.

A FIELD

Donkeys are nibbling grass as teen-age boys in overalls climb a fence to play ball. Charlie and another miner, plus girls in Depression dresses, stop at the fence and watch as the biggest boy hollers and starts chasing the donkeys with the bat. One of them stops abruptly and aims a kick at the kid's chest, knocking him tumbling backwards while the onlookers double with laughter.

"Man, look at that mule kick!" . . . .

The kid picks himself up, throws his bat at the beast, chases it out of the field, and slams the gate shut. Then he angrily tosses a ball in the air and smacks it after the animal galloping out of sight.

When he limps back, Charlie and his buddy, another miner, Mountain Man Hubbard, are still laughing. "Heh, Mule, let me see that muscle!" The Man feels it admiringly. "Whyn't you come out to the men's team? We're gonna play Casey Stengel and some of his boys Saturday. Make a little dough."

A MINOR LEAGUE LOCKER ROOM

Guys are tucking in uniforms, adjusting jock straps, pulling up socks etc. The door opens a few inches, and Mule peeks in. He starts to retreat quickly, but the skipper, called "Mountain," spots him. "Heh, c'mere, Kid!" He pulls the boy in as the others look up curiously. "Here's our new left fielder!" he shouts while Mule tries to hide behind him. "Here!" Mountain shoves a uniform bundle at him.

Mule retreats to the farthest corner he can find and slowly begins un-buttoning his shirt. The uniform sleeves come down to his finger tips. He rolls them up. He pulls on the pants, and they hang below his feet. He has to roll them up too. The belt is too long and dangles limply after he tightens it to the last hole. The cap comes down over one ear and both eyes. Mountain shakes his head and gets a safety pin to pin it tighter. The others watch out of the corners of their eyes and can't suppress their chuckles.

MINOR LEAGUE FIELD

A loudspeaker plays "The Sunny Side of the Street" ("Get your coat and get your hat, leave your worries on the door step.") The grandstand is filled with white men in straw hats and vests and women in 1930s permanent waves. The bleachers are filled with blacks - coal miners in coveralls, women in gingham dresses, boys in knickers.

A white team wearing the uniforms of "CASEY STENGEL'S ALL STARS" is taking infield practice, snapping throws around the bases.

A black team, wearing the striped flannels of the "KEYSTONES," trots out of the dugout.

The last player hesitates on the dugout steps. He is wearing a gray uniform several sizes too large. He wears sneakers instead of baseball shoes. Finally, he ducks his head down and hurries out, trying to look inconspicuous. But the crowd spots him anyway and points and laughs.

An announcer with a megaphone walks to home plate.

ANNOUNCER

"The manager of the Major All Stars - Casey Stengel!

Amid applause Casey hobbles spryly to the plate, a mischievous grin on his face.

"Ladies and gentlemen. Today we got with us the greatest pitcher in America, the man who won 31 games for the Philadelphia Athletics - Lefty Grove!"

With a flourish he points to the dugout, where Grove appears, his cap raised, to loud applause. He trots to the mound, kicks high, and delivers a fastball - <u>whap</u>!

"And now, the man you've all been waitin' for - home run champeen of the world - the one, the only - BABE RUTH!"

The cheers are thunderous as Ruth, now at the end of his career and showing a paunch, lumbers onto the field, whirling three bats around his shoulders. He discards two, then slowly points to the fence. He holds the pose as the cheers roll in.

CASEY

"May the best team win. I thank you for your kind attention."

He sweeps his cap off and bows low as a bird flies off his head to great laughter.

In the blacks' dugout Mountain turns to his pitcher. "You know who everyone came to see, right?"

The hurler nods.

"So no funny business. Got it?"

"Got it. right down the pike."

A slap of the rump, and he trots to the mound.

Ruth steps to the plate. A mighty swing, and the ball climbs into the sky and disappears beyond the fence to a roar from the crowd.

Next inning Grove waits as Mule shyly up to bat. The ball comes in

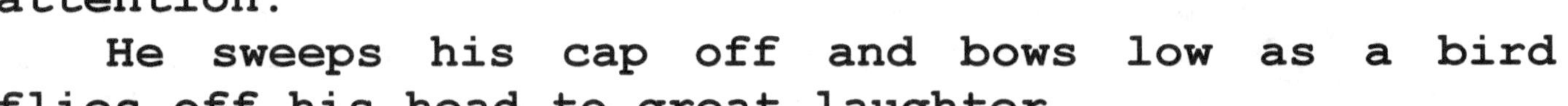

under chin, and he falls back on the dirt. He brushes himself off and gets back in the batter's box. On the next pitch he drills a shot that spins the shortstop around.

The fans in the bleachers cheer:

"Way to go!... Kick, Mule!"

One fan, Charlie, jumps to his feet despite his crutches.

"That's my boy, Mule! That's my brother!"

He clasps his hands above his head and grins broadly to all sides.

Several girls wave and call.

"Heh, Mister Mule. You gonna hit one   out for us?"

The players (mimicking): "Heh, lover boy, You gonna hit one out for us?"

They guffaw.

Coming up again, Mule rips a low line drive to center, so hard that it scoots through the fielder's legs. As Mule rounds first, his hat falls down over his eyes. Foxx playfully grabs his belt, and Mule's pants sag toward his knees. He trips on them and stumbles as the outfielder chases the ball. Mule rounds second without touching the base, scrambles back and tags it, then heads for third. The girls pour over the bleacher railing and run the field. Mule sees them, slams on the brakes, and dives back into second head-first just ahead of the ball.

FANS

"Man! Look at the Mule kick!"

On his third at bat, Mule hits a savage drive to third. The third baseman leaps, but the ball flies into leftfield, taking his glove along with it. The bleacher fans laugh and clap.

On Mule's fourth at bat, the infielders have backed up into the outfield. The outfielders are touching the fence.

THIRD BASEMAN

"Keep it outside to him, man!"

FIRST BASEMAN

(Laughing): "Make him pull it, dammit!"

SHORTSTOP

"Don't give him anything low! Make him hit it in the air."

PITCHER

"What are _you_ all scared of? Look where you are! I'm just sixty feet away from him!"

Stengel trots to the mound.

"What do _you_ want me to do, Skip? Curve or fastball?"

"I don't know, son. Just pitch and pray."

With a pat of the rump, Casey trots back to the dugout. The hurler pitches, and he and the infielders immediately dive for the ground. Mule is so surprised, he laughs and misses the ball.

OUTSIDE THE PARK

Babe and Casey are signing autographs. Mule walks past, followed by ten or 12 kids, calling, "Can I carry your bat, Mule?. . . Can I carry your glove?"

CASEY

"Good hittin', young fella."

BABE

"I'm glad you're not in the American League!"

"Aw, you shoulda seen my brother."

CASEY

(Eagerly:) "Which one was _he_?"

"Naw, he can't play. He busted his leg in the mine."

"How'd you like to play _real_ baseball? For money?"

"What you mean, 'real' baseball? You know they won't let us in the big leagues."

"I mean Negro baseball. You know why they call me Casey?"

Mule shakes his head.

"'Cause I come from K.C. You ever hear of the Kansas City Monarchs?"

Mule shakes his head again.

"Well, they got some of the best ball players in America. I know, 'cause I found half of 'em. How'd you like to play for them?"

"I don't know.... I can't leave my job."

"Job! How much you making?"

"Twenty-five dollars a month."

"If you don't break a leg."

"It's better'n washin' windows."

"How'd you like to make fifty?"

Mule's eyes open wide.

"Fifty dollars!"

"I got a friend, J.L. Wilkinson, owns the Kansas City Monarchs. I'm gonna tell him about you. Interested?"

Is he!

"But I gotta ask my momma first."

He thinks of a question. "Do they play in Chicago?"

"Sure."

"What about New York?"

"(Amused:) "Hell yes, they do."

(Suspiciously:) "How about California?"

Casey thinks. "Yeah, in the winter."

"Oh, man, I want to see California!"

Mule leaps and runs off, followed by the boys. He stops and joyfully hits a fungo grounder to his little army. They pitch it back to Mule, who pretends to miss it. After a few swings, Mule offers one boy the bat and tosses an underhand pitch to him. The boys are all chattering and yelling.

"Me next, Mule.... Let me hit!"

Around a corner the girls appear and catch sight of him and break into a run. Mule turns and dashes off in the other direction, followed by the boys, and after them, the girls.

Casey shakes his head and smiles.

You ever see anything like him, Jimmie?"

(Laughing:): "He's the biggest kid out there!"

They shake their heads and walk toward their bus.

MINE ENTRANCE

We hear "Stormy Weather" ("Don't know why ain't no sun up in the sky") as the mine elevator door opens, disgorging miners. Mule and Charlie shuffle out and start trudging home. Charlie is limping.

MULE

"Oh, Lord, there's got to be a better life than this. How'm I ever gonna get out of this damn mine?"

Behind them a limousine stops at the foreman's shack, and a man leans out to ask directions. He waves a thank you, and the car drives past Mule and Charlie, its Missouri license plate visible in the swirling dust.

MULE

"You know where that car's goin', Charlie?"

"No, Mule, where?"

"To our home."

"How do you know that?"

"I just know it"

UNPAVED STREET OF MINERS' SHACKS

Mule and Charlie spot the car in front of their house. Charlie is amazed. They mount the porch steps. The boys walk in to find Momma and two strangers - one extends his hand.

"Hi, my name's Oscar Charleston. The Kansas City Monarchs."

The boys gulp and exchange looks. They know all about Charleston, called "the greatest black player ever - New

York Giants' manager John McGraw called hIm "the greatest player, period."

"And this here is Bullet Joe Rogan."

The boys' eyes bug out. Rogan stands only 5'6", but in his heyday, a decade ago, he was the greatest pitcher in Negro League baseball - some said, in all baseball.

CHARLESTON

"I guess you heard about how he struck out Babe Ruth back in 'twenty-four?"

The guys are so thunder-struck they stammer, trying to get out their names. Bullet Joe shakes cordially and addresses Charlie, the bigger and older of the two. "Mule, we've heard a lot about you."

CHARLIE

"Uh, I'm Charles. This here is my baby brother. We call him Mule, 'cause he hits like a Mule kicks."

They look down at Charlie's twisted foot, and there is an awkward silence.

BULLET JOE

"Oh. I'm sorry."

CHARLIE

"No need to be, Mister Rogan. Nobody can hit 'em like Mule, he's gonna be great some day."

"Well, we heard how he can hit. And we think he'd be a big help to the Monarchs. We'd like you to play for us, son. What do you say?"

Mule looks at Momma.

"No use asking him does he want to go. That's all he talks about is seeing New York and California and all those places."

CHARLESTON

"Well, then, do we have a deal?"

MOMMA

"Just a minute, Mister Cooper. George is only eighteen. He's never been outside this state. He don't know anything about those places. Are you gonna take care of him and make sure he goes to church every Sunday?"

"Oh yes ma'am. Mister Wilkinson is the owner, and Candy Jim Taylor is the manager. They're both good Christian gentlemen. We'll all take good care of him."

"Well, if you're sure ..."

"I promise you, Miz Samson."

Momma studies his face. At length –

"... Then I guess he can go."

Mule's face lights up like a candle. Momma gives him a big hug. All shake his hand, none more vigorously than Charlie.

CHARLESTON

"We pay fifty dollars on the first of every month, come hell – er, heck – or high water."

He peels off five two-dollar bills and hands them to Momma. "This is for his bus to Kansas City. We'll meet him at the depot next Tuesday morning.

"Welcome to the team, Mule."

After Charleston and Rogan leave, Momma, Mule, and Charlie stand looking at each other.

MOMMA

"What's he gonna wear? He doesn't have a suit."

CHARLIE

"He can have my suit. It's a little big on him, but you can take it in."

MULE

"That's for your wedding, Charlie."

"Don't you worry about that. I'll get another one. This is your big chance, boy. You got to grab it."

Charlie goes into a bedroom and takes a white shirt from the closet. Then pulls an old suitcase from under the bed.

"Here. Put your things in this."

Mule murmurs thank you. "You should be going instead me ..."

'Don't worry about me, boy. You saved my life. I'm gonna be proud of you."

KANSAS PRAIRIE, 1936

The "Sons of the Pioneers" sing "Tumbling Tumble Weeds" as a black team poses proudly before their Ford touring car, along with bearded white House of David players, who stand and kneel among them. The photo gradually assumes color, and the players come to life. They shake hands with the House of Davids, wave good-bye, and begin piling into their car and a bus.

Jud is built like a rassler, with broad shoulders. He speaks gruffly in a <u>basso</u> voice: "Heh, Busher, pick up my uniform roll!"

Mule already has his own roll on one shoulder. He stoops and hoists Jud's, but two of his bats fall off. He tries to catch them, but loses first Jud's roll, then his own. The players watch and chuckle.

JUD

"Dumb kid. Don't know nothin'. How's he expect to make this team?"

A young player, Cool, comes over to help. He holds Jud's bag while Mule hoists his own, then helps him put Jud's on the other shoulder. Mule stumbles but carries them to the car, losing another bat as he goes, to a new round of laughter. He shrugs both burdens onto the car roof, ties them down, retrieves the bat and secures it, grinning sheepishly.

COOL

(Whispering:) "Watch out for Jud, kid. He's mean enough to go bear huntin' with a switch. Don't need no gun."

Mule starts to climb in front. Jud pulls him roughly by the collar.

"Where the hell you think you're goin'"?

Jud takes the passenger seat beside J.L. Wikinson, the team owner. Wilkie is a short, rotund man in shirtsleeves and vest with a derby hat. He's been traveling these prairies for 15 years, leading his black players from town to town, from Montana to Mexico and back.

Mule squeezes into the back seat, where three men are already sitting. They grunt and half-heartedly make a little room. Wilkie puts the car in gear, it coughs, lurches, and begins a top-heavy ride onto a rural road. It is followed by a bus, emblazoned with a sign,

KANSAS CITY MONARCHS
KINGS OF COLORED BASEBALL

and a Ford pickup truck filled with lighting equipment. The caravan slowly chugs toward the horizon.

In the bus the players reach down and pull out cardboard boxes from under their seats and extract bread, cold cuts, mustard, Cokes, and beer, and begin making a meal.

SMALL KANSAS TOWN

Evening is approaching. The sound track plays Bing Crosby crooning, "When the deep purple falls (over sleepy garden walls)." A festival atmosphere prevails. Kids and adults make way for the Monarchs, who pile out of their cars and bus to join the stream of people going toward a county fair bleachers. Kids in knickers rush to carry gloves, bats, etc. Men in overalls carry youngsters on their shoulders. Farm wives offer the players baskets of fried chicken, biscuits, etc. The pied pipers file into the park, signing autographs as they walk.

The players and town men pitch in to unload the truck, erect the light poles around the bleachers and hook them to a generator while men and boys police the field, picking up cow chips.

The generator coughs, and the lights blink on, to the ooh's of the crowd.

In the bus Bobby, an 18 year-old white pitcher, busily applies shoe polish to his face.

A new, shiny bus arrives with a sign,
PITTSBURGH CRAWFORDS,
NEGRO WORLD CHAMPIONS

The players - Satchel Paige, Josh Gibson, and others - emerge to cheers, sign autographs, and begin warming up. Josh smashes some gigantic blasts into the trees beyond centerfield, then over the trees. At each one, the crowd erupts with applause.

On the sidelines, players play "pepper." Standing in a circle, they toss a ball to each other with trick throws over their shoulders, between their legs etc, and catch it behind their backs, or make the ball pop out of their gloves as the fans laugh.

Satchel, tall and gangly, is warming up to pitch. He is the most famous pitcher in black baseball, perhaps the best pitcher in the country of any color. He surveys the world with a twinkling eye as if he has just thought of a good joke.

Josh, the catcher, holds up a board with a knothole. He inserts the ball into the hole to show the crowd that the ball just does fit, and tosses it to Satch. The big pitcher winds up and throws. The ball rolls around and drops back out. He throws another, and this time it goes through without touching the sides, as Satchel raises his hands triumphantly and smiles broadly to more clapping and cheering.

The Monarchs have put on clown uniforms over their baseball gear. Some wear grass skirts, others are in conical hats, ruffled collars, over-sized shoes, putty noses, etc.

Mule heads for third base to find Jud already there.

JUD

"You want to make this team, kid, you better go over there."

He points to first base with his chin. Mule shrugs, trots across the diamond, finds Candy Jim, the manager, at the bag, and sits on the sidelines to watch. Candy is nearing 40 and carries a bit of a paunch. He's a popular, fatherly leader.

The better slaps a fungo to begin a fancy-dan infield practice, with sensational catches by Jud, shortstop Skinny, and second baseman Ramon, a nimble Cuban.

Ramon wears a read bandana and bracelets, which he shakes often.

Skinny is short and lithe, the team cut-up, full of mischief and practical jokes.

In the midst of the routine, first baseman Buck turns his back to look at the crowd as Jud unleashes a hard throw straight at him. While the horrified crowd gasps and shouts a warning, at the last second Buck nonchalantly puts his glove in the small of his back, and the ball smacks into it.

Candy pretends to toss a ball into the air and hit it.

Skinny scoots to his right and pretends to make a sensational backhand catch and off-balance throw. Ramon "takes" the throw at second, leaps to avoid an imaginary base runner's spikes, and relays it to first. There Buck stretches and makes a beautiful one-hop swipe.

Laughter and clapping greet the play.

Jimmy, the left fielder, sneaks behind Jud at third base. Every move Jud makes is mirrored by Jimmy. Jud moves to his left; Jim is in perfect step behind him. Jud punches his glove; so does Jim. Jud puts his hands on his knees; Jim is his shadow.

The crowd titters. Jud looks surprised, looks to left and right but can't see the cause of the mirth. Jim also looks to left and right. Both shrug.

Candy hits a sharp but invisible grounder to third. Jud dashes in and bare-hands it. Jimmy is right behind him. Jud whips a throw to home. Only then does he notice Jimmy also throwing home. In mock anger, he chases Jim to the outfield, where Jim leaps and falls over the fence just in the nick of time.

The crowd loves it.

Dobie carries a rocking chair out to home plate and sits down. He takes a candle and candle-holder from inside his shirt, lights the candle, and places it on his head. Benny winds up and pitches a real ball, knocking the candle off without touching Dobie. The crowd applauds.

As the public address plays Hoagie Carmichael singing "Old rockin' chair's got me." Dobie rocks lazily, Benny pitches, and Dobie casually gloves it. Jimmy, on first base, digs toward second, and Dobie, without missing a beat on the rocker, throws him out.

Buck comes to bat and hits a long drive that disappears above the lights. Cool, in center field, turns and runs to the base of the tree, his cap flying off, turns again, and the ball magically reappears just where he is standing.

The crowd claps.

On the next pitch, Buck swings again and hits a hard foul tip, which smacks Dobie in the chest, knocking him backwards. He does a double-roll on the ground as the Monarchs run off the field to loud applause.

ANNOUNCER

"Now the Monarchs will show us how they play their world-famous "donkey ball!"

MULE

"<u>What</u> kinda ball?"

He is about to get his answer as farmers lead seven donkeys onto the field. The Monarchs, who have done this before, run out to their donkeys.

ANNOUNCER

"Folks, the first batter up is a real Mule!"

MULE

"Oh no! I never rode one of them things in my life!"

CANDY

"Don't worry, Kid. The donkey does all the work." He gives Mule a push onto the field.

The public address plays "Donkey Serenade" as Mule clumps to the plate in over-size clown shoes, ruffled collar, and putty nose. He looks warily at the donkey being held beside home plate.

ANNOUNCER

"Okay, folks, most of you know the rules. The catcher and batter take their usual positions. Everyone else is on a donkey. They'll have to ride it to catch the ball and ride around the bases.

Mule steps in the box. Mac, the Monarchs' relief pitcher, lobs an easy pitch, which Mule smashes into left-center.

Cool and Benny, the leftfielder, spur their beasts, both of which balk and bray. Cool gets off and tries to pull his. Benny kicks furiously but fruitlessly. He gets off and tries to push his steed. It kicks, sending Ben sprawling on his rump.

The crowd roars and laughs.

Mule tries to mount but isn't sure how.

CROWD

"Don't be afraid, Mule!... Show him who's boss!"

Mule jumps but can't hold onto the donkey's back. The crowd roars. He tries to get a leg over his beast. He fails. His hat falls over his face in the attempt. He tries again, and gets one ankle over, tugging and pulling on the donkey's mane while kicking with his free leg. He finally struggles up and slides head-first off the other side.

The announcer holds a piece of cloth in front of his mike and slowly rips.

Mule assumes his own pants have sprung a tear and grabs his behind with one hand. The crowd breaks up.

Finally, the farmer gives Mule a leg up onto his steed. Mule kicks his heels into the donkey's flanks. Nothing happens.

Meanwhile Cool has pulled his mount to six inches from the ball. He holds the reins with one hand and strains forward with the other. He is inches shy. The harder he pulls, the more the donkey balks, and the louder the laughs.

Mule's beast finally begins sauntering toward the dugout. Mule tugs on one rein and turns the donkey in a full circle.

Benny meanwhile has gotten back on his mount, which is munching grass.

As the crowd eggs Mule on, his beast, suddenly kicks, almost throwing Mule off to the side. The donkey bucks again, and Mule throws both arms around its neck.

ANNOUNCER

"Ride 'im, cowboy!"

A scratchy recording of "I'm an old' cowhand (from the Riot Grande)"." The crowd roars even louder.

Cool finally reaches the ball and throws it to the infield. Skinny kicks his mount furiously to reach it.

Mule's mount suddenly decides to run. Mule hangs on with both hands around the neck, his rump bumping up and down. Just before reaching the bag, however, the donkey puts on the brakes. Mule, bug-eyed with fright, is vaulted over the donkey's head, somersaulting to a hard landing on his back on top of the bag.

His breath knocked out of him, Mule slowly gets up to applause, slaps the dust off his hat against his thigh, and begins an exaggerated bow-legged rodeo cowhand's limp to the dugout. The crowd loves it.

The Monarchs run into the dugout, playfully punching Mule.

They doff their clown uniforms.

CANDY JIM

"Okay, boys, that's enough messin' around. Now let's play some baseball."

Satchel is on the mound as Cool steps up, tapping the plate with his bat.

MULE

(To Candy:) "What does this guy throw?"

"Man, don't you know who that is? That's Satchel Paige. He doesn't throw but one thing."

Satchel's right arm goes around in a windmill motion, he lifts his foot high, revealing the words "FASTBALL" on the sole, and delivers. The ball, unseen, thumps into Josh's mitt.

UMPIRE

"Strike!"

Cool scratches his head.

"That sounded a little low didn't it, ump?"

Josh holds up the ball for everyone to see, and throws it back. The fans laugh, and Satchel breaks into a big grin. Cool looks at two more invisible strikes.

Skinny, the next batter, takes three swings and misses. Ramon also strikes out and walks away muttering as the fans laugh even louder and Satchel boogies off the mound.

BUCK

(Nodding to Mule:) "I don't feel so good tonight, Kid. You better play first base."

The players laugh.

Bobby, a teen-age white in blackface, takes the mound for the Monarchs. The first Crawford batter flies out to Cool. The second misses three pitches.

The third batter grounds to third, where Jud waits for it with open arms. It smacks him in the chest and drops to the ground. He picks it up fires the ball to Mule at first. Mule gets his feet tangled up touching the bag and is spiked in the ankle. The Craws razz him. He trots to the dugout, pretending he isn't hurt, but his socks are slowly filling with blood.

JUD

"Dumb busher! Gonna get himself killed."

Jud swings three bats around his head with one hand, throws two away, and steps into the batter's box. He takes a big swing and the ball sails to the opposite field, whacking the fence.

CANDY

(Yukking merrily to Mule:) "Hear that ball go 'boo-jum'?" He cups his hands and shouts. "Way to go, Boojum!"

Mule is selecting a bat.

"OK, boy, you're up. Don't let him scare you. Don't swing at every one. Wait for one you can hit." He gives Mule a slap on the rump as Mule walks apprehensively up to bat.

The Crawfords begin filing their spikes. They look across the diamond and yell, "This is for you, Busher."

JOSH

"Man, these lights are pretty dim, boy. Even _I_ don't know where that ball's goin'. You better stay loose."

Satchel whirls his arm and fires down the middle. Mule offers at it awkwardly for a strike. On the second pitch, Satchel throws sidearm, and Mule falls back from an inside pitch. The third pitch comes in at Mule's head. He backs away again, but the ball curves over for strike three.

SATCHEL

(Laughing:) "They told you I didn't have a curve, didn't they, kid? Well, I was savin' that one for you."

CANDY

"Why didn't you do what I told you?"

MULE

"I _did_, but he didn't _throw_ something I could hit."

Candy motions Mule to pick up a glove and follow him behind the stands. "Here, kid, you got to move like this."

He demonstrates a hop to his left, then a hop to his right.

"Now you try it.

Mule tries it and trips over himself. "Aw, they're paying me to hit home runs, not to catch balls.

Candy: "Well, I can <u>see</u> that."

Mule comes up a second time. He winds his bat and waits. He lines a long drive to left, but it hooks foul. He gets a small piece of the next pitch and fouls it back.

Satchel gives him a big windup motion and strides. Mule swings. Satchel completes the follow-through, and the ball floats over for strike three.

CANDY

"Oh-oh. I should have told him about Satchel's hesitation pitch."

LATER

Bobby pitching. A runner on first. Josh smashes a hard grounder into the hole between short and third. Skinny scoots far to his right in short leftfield and bare-hands the ball. He makes a half-spin and backhands the ball to Jud at third. Jud whips it to second to start a double play.

ANNOUNCER

"How 'bout that, folks? They could turn a double play with a <u>frog</u>!"

Sixth inning, the Craws lead 1-0. Jud smites a drive to the base of the trees for a double, and Mule comes to bat again. He misses a high ball, looks at Cool in the first-base coaching box. Cool claps and nods encouragement.

Mule hits the next one hard. The outfielder backs up as the ball disappears half-way up in the branches. Mule jogs around the bases behind Jud, beaming.

The Monarchs clap and slap their thighs.

"Man, look at that Mule kick... Yeah, he sure kicked that one! ... Kick, Mule! Kick it, boy!"

Jud and Mule trot into the dugout.

MULE

"How 'bout <u>that</u>, old man? Bet you never hit one that far in your life." Jud whirls around, fists doubled. Mule sucks in his breath, stands his ground. The players watch the two glare at each other.

JUD

"Shoot, man, you shoulda seen me when I <u>really</u> could hit."

Jud walks away, muttering, "Dumb kid can't hit a curve."

Skinny wanders down to the third base coaching box and speaks into an imaginary telephone.

"Hello? Honey?... How ya doin' You say you're in bed?... With who?... Oh, your sister. . . I thought the ice man just dropped by."

The fans guffaw.

Next Skinny pantomimes a crap game. He rolls the "dice," pops his eyes with glee, and rakes in the pot. He shakes and rolls again with a snap of his fingers and rakes in another pot. The crowd titters. He pushes his winnings back in the pot, pauses, removes his shoes and puts them in too, then his cap, his shirt, and his belt. He starts to remove his trousers, but suddenly notices the fans and quickly pulls his pants back up. He points to the pot for the others to match it.

Satisfied, he rolls again - and stares in shock. His face contorts, and he rolls on the ground, as the fans go wild.

Ninth inning. Mule is at bat again. A new pitcher, a big Indian named Smoky Joe, is on the mound.

JOSH

"You hit pretty good for a dumb-ass kid. Let's see if you can hit with the ball in your mouth."

In slow motion Joe raises his leg and delivers a sidearm pitch that comes in high and inside, straight at Mule's head. Mule ducks too late. The ball hits with a loud crack, and the screen goes blank.

Jud charges out with a bat, bellowing curses. Josh turns to intercept him. Jud's teammates grab him from behind.

MULE'S POV

The screen slowly focuses. Candy Jim's face slowly swims into view.

"How many fingers can you see, Kid?"

(Weakly:) "... "Two?

"Can you see first base?"

Mule tries to focus. "Uh... yeah."

"Well, get up and get on it."

Candy trots back to the dugout. Mule totters toward third, hesitates, gets himself turned around, and wobbles to first.

The game is over, and both teams trot off the field.

ANNOUNCER

And now, ladies and gentleman, for your delectation and enjoyment, the Monarchs of Music will play for your dancing pleasure.

At a nearby outdoor bandstand, the players, still in uniform, take seats and unlimber their instruments. Ramon plays the guitar, Candy Jim the cornet, Dobie a banjo, Bobby an accordion, Skinny a trombone, and Skinny taps out the rhythm on the bones.

CANDY

"You play anything, Mule?"

He shakes his head.

"Do you sing?"

"Uh-uh."

"Okay. Here." he hands him two spoons. "Hold 'em like this" - he demonstrates. "Then just tap them on you leg." He taps out a rhythm. Mule fumbles, and the spoons won't stay in place. He makes a face and tries again.

The little orchestra strikes up "Red Sails in the Sunset (way out on the sea)", and couples, old and young, begin the two-step beneath the moon. Mule is still struggling with the spoons.

A quartet — Skinny is tenor, Cool and Buck sing baritone, and Jud is bass — chime in with a perfect imitation of the Ink Spots: "If I didn't know (why the roses grow."

Next the band swings into something faster, Duke Ellington's "Take the A-Train," for the younger people while Candy does a cornet solo. Mule gets the hang of it, and begins furiously tapping, first on one leg, then the other. A wide smile lights his face.

They switch to Hoagy Carmichael's "Stardust" ("Beside a garden wall...") as the singers harmonize.

Then all the dancers take the floor as the quartet sings a dreamy "Goodnight, Sweetheart ('till we meet tomorrow)." The camera slowly pulls away, as one by one the lights on the bandstand go out.

IN THE BUS

Wilkie counts the day's receipts. Jud reaches under his seat, gets a miner's helmet, and tosses it to Mule.

"Here, this may save your life."

The others chuckle. Mule looks it over, claps it on his head, and knocks it with his knuckle. He nods a thank you.

Bobby is trying to scrub the shoe polish off his face.

BOBBY

"How do you get this damn stuff off?"

CANDY

(Softly): "I wish I knew, son. I wish I knew."

LOBBY, SMALL TOWN HOTEL

Music: "It was only a paper moon (floating over a cardboard sea." Wilkinson and the players stand at the front desk. A few locals in bib overalls sit in rocking chairs in the empty lobby. A noisy fan whirs. Wilkie is addressing the clerk, who wears garters on his sleeves and mops the sweat from his face.

WILKIE

".. . What do you mean, 'full?" I wrote Sam Johnson we were coming. We've been staying here for twenty years."

CLERK

"I'm sorry, sir, there's been an error.

"Error? Where's Sam? Tell him I want to see him."

"Mister Johnson sold out last winter. I'm sorry, I wish I could help."

With a scowl, Wilkie leads the team out.

A VICTORIAN HOME

Wilkie and the players climb the porch steps and ring the doorbell as the sound track plays "Two sleepy people." The porch light comes on, and a man answers. He is one of the men who had clamored for an autograph before the game.

WILKIE

"Sorry to trouble you, sir, but we've had a little misunderstanding at the hotel, and my players haven't got anywhere to sleep tonight. I don't suppose you would have a room. I'll be glad to pay you."

The man eyes them all slowly. "Uh, okay. I guess we can help. How 'bout you?"

He points to Bobby, who hesitates and looks around at the others.

PLAYERS

"Go ahead, Bobby... Don't worry about us... We'll be okay."

Bobby shakes his head. "Naw, that's okay. If you don't sleep, I don't sleep. Thanks anyway, mister."

The man nods and closes the door. The light goes out.

At another home, Wilkie rings. The door opens, then closes as the men turn and walk away and the light goes out.

Next they try the jail. The sergeant greets them with his feet on the desk.

WILKIE

"Sorry to bother you, but we had a problem at the hotel, and...

"Don't worry about a thing. We can put three of you up here." He takes the keys down from the wall, saunters into the back, and opens a cell door, revealing four bunks, one with a drunk snoring on it.

"It's not great, but old Bill seems to be enjoying it.

RAMON

"Mon, we take it!"

Skinny apprehensively follows Ramon in. The sergeant swings the door shut and turns the key.

SKINNY

"Heh, wait a minute!"

WILKIE

(Waving:) "'Night, boys. I'll bail you out in the morning."

FUNERAL HOME

The funeral sign is lit on the lawn. Willkie rings the bell as the players hang back, shaking their heads.

SKINNY

(With bravado): "Heck, I ain't scared."

DOBIE

"Me - me neither."

They follow Wilkie as he rings the bell. The funeral director in bathrobe, answers, listens, smiles, and beckons them in. Jimmy pushes Ben, who pushes back, then both hesitantly enter.

They follow through the dimly-lit hallway, peering curiously into the rooms, one with an open casket and banks of flowers. The director leads them down creaky stairs to a store room with a few more caskets and two couches.

"I'm sorry, this is all I've got. But it should be comfortable. . . And very quiet."

He hands them blankets. "Have a pleasant night."

They watch him climb back up the stairs and close the door on creaking hinges. Alone, they look at each other and pull the covers up, but their eyes dart nervously.

BUS DEPOT

Fly-specked posters of Franklin Roosevelt and Alf Landon, his presidential opponent, adorn one wall, a Chesterfield cigarette ad and a movie poster of Charlie Chaplin's "City Lights" are on another.

TICKET CLERK

"Well, we're not supposed to, but, sure, won't do no harm."

Wilkie, Candy, and Bobby wearily slump on the hard wooden benches and adjust their jackets under their heads.

JUD

"I'm gonna drive tonight. See you all in Tulsa tomorrow. Anybody coming with me?"

Cool, Skinny, Buck, and Mule turn to the door.
                              WILKIE

"Drive careful."

He fluffs his jacket under his head and pulls his hat down over his eyes.

Outside, the Ford is parked by the team bus beneath the lamp-lit Greyhound sign. Mule climbs sleepily into the back seat.
                               JUD

"Bushers drive!"

Mule gets up front, the other four get in - Jud in front - and Mule noisily puts the car into gear. It lurches forward across a curb, backs up to the sound of stripping gears, and clips a garbage can before he finally gets it straightened out. Jud rolls his eyes nervously.

                        COUNTRY HIGHWAY

The car speeds along, weaving behind two circles of headlights.

In the back seat, Buck begins to sing quietly. "I'd climb the highest mountain..."

Jud chimes in: "If I knew that when I climbed that mountain,

Cool and Skinny pick it up: "I'd find you."

Mule bashfully joins them, off-key, until the others scowl. Soon the rest are harmonizing like the Mills Brothers.

The voices waft into the night as the car moves under the prairie moon.

The players fall asleep, each man in the back has his head on the shoulder of the man on his left.

Mule nods at the wheel. He wanders into the headlights of an oncoming car and swerves just in time.

Buck opens one eye and mumbles: Shift." Without waking, the three turn their heads to rest on the man to the right.

The car drones on, behind its headlights.

PART II

1933

HIGHWAY, NIGHT
The headlights pick small blue signs with white letters every 100 feet:
Old grandpa's beard...
Was stiff and coarse...
The reason for...
His fifth divorce...
Burma Shave

Mule skids to a stop at a neon sign and two Richfield gas pumps. The flickering sign reads
HAMB RGERS 5c
GAS 10.9c a gal
Jud rouses himself, looks around.
MULE
"I'm hungry."
"Yeah, let's get some hamburgers." He pushes Skinny awake. "You go in - take my hat."
Skinny pulls the cap low and shuffles to the door. The others head for the bushes away from the light.
Inside, the waitress is smoking, leafing through "The Saturday Evening Post." The radio plays, "I got a right to sing the blues." The place is empty of customers. She barely looks up.
"Yeah?"
"Fifteen hamburgers and five Cokes to go."
She calls over her shoulder: "Fifteen 'burgers to go," and resumes reading.
Outside, Mule hops out of the bushes, buttoning his fly.
"Heh, I want a pie too!" He dashes in the door. Cool starts to yell, "Wait!" but it's too late.
WAITRESS
"Heh, you can't come in here!"
Skinny suddenly turns the other way and scratches his cheek.
"He with you?"

Skinny smiles innocently and shakes his head. She takes a closer look at him. "Get out! Both of you! I'll call the cops."

The cook hands a bag of hamburgers through the window.

Skinny takes the two dollars off the counter and puts it back in his pocket. "I hope you all have a good time eating all them hamburgers you cooked."

"Heh, wait a minute! Come back! You can't go!"

Cool and Skinny jump into the car, followed by the others, still buttoning up.

Dawn is breaking to the music of "Two Sleepy people by dawn's early light." Mule nods and blinks awake just as an oncoming car appears over the crest of a hill, its bright headlights suddenly blinding him. He pulls on the wheel just in time. The players are jolted awake.

SKINNY

"Heh, you want me to drive?"

MULE

Drowsy: "Yeah, okay."

He starts to pull over, but the brake pedal goes to the floor. The car picks up speed as Mule furiously pumps the useless brake. Everyone is awake now and shouting as the car careens faster and faster toward a village at the foot of the hill.

A horse-drawn wagon slowly clops across the highway ahead of them. Mule furiously honks, and every man shouts in horror and jams his own foot helplessly on the floor.

Mule desperately pulls the wheel to the right to pass behind the wagon, but the driver tugs quickly on the reins, the horse rears and neighs in the path of the on-rushing car. At the last second Mule swerves to the left and passes under the hooves of the pawing, whinnying horse.

The car almost overturns, but screeches back upright, smashes through a rail fence, jumps a ditch, ploughs through a hedge, smacks into a corner of a shed, leaps over a trough, and lands with a splash in the middle of a sty as the pigs run, squealing in terror.

Slowly the men push the doors open and climb unsteadily out. They struggle through ankle-deep mud and collapse on the ground, moaning and rubbing their bones while the radiator spouts steam like Old Faithful.

COOL

"Heh, where's Mule at?"

They look around, but he's nowhere to be seen. Jud gingerly picks his way back through the muck and peers inside the car.

JUD

"C'mere.... Man, look at the kid!

The others look inside. There is Mule in the driver's seat, glassy-eyed, his fingers still tightly clutching the wheel, which he has wrenched completely off.

Jud grabs Mule under the arms, pulls him out, and sits him down on a dry spot. Then with some effort he and Buck pry his fingers loose from the wheel.

BUCK

"Man, he's got a grip like my old lady!"

A Menonite farmer and his wife appear. He's pulling on his suspenders, she's tucking up her hair. They survey the scene.

FARMER

"Well, lookee that!"

The players begin scraping the mud off their clothes. "You boys all right?"

JUD

"Sorry about this, Mister. The brakes gave out on us."

FARMER

"Well, praise the Lord you're okay. (Shakes his head.) I don't know how in the world you missed the pigs!"

JUD

"We'll be glad to pay for the damage, sir."

The farmer studies the scene.

FARMER

"Well, I was gonna knock that shed down anyway. I'll have to mend the fence. Tell you what I'll do." He kicks the tires. "You give me the car and five dollars, and we'll call it even."

Jud reaches into his pocket and pulls out four one-dollar bills. He finds some change in the other pocket and counts it out into the farmer's hand.

"We're much obliged to you, mister."

The farmer turns to his wife. "Mother, think you can get these boys some scrambled eggs and a little bacon?"

The players return their empty plates and wave goodbye.

BUCK

"How we gonna get to Tulsa now, Jud?"

"Shut up and follow me!" (To Mule:) "Pick up my bag! Let's go."

They trudge off behind him toward a railroad track in the distance. Mule is almost lost under two uniform rolls.

The lights of a town are seen in the distance. A freight train lumbers by, and five bags come flying out, followed by five men, rolling and stumbling as they hit the ground. They dust themselves off, find their bags, and head for trees at a nearby creek.

A HOBO JUNGLE

some white hoboes squat around a fire, stirring a soup can of water. One is playing a harmonica: "I'll never smile again (until I smile at you...)"

JUD

"Hi, boys."

They grunt and nod.

"Got any grub for some hungry guys?"

FIRST HOBO

"Sure. Plenty. Same place we got ours." He nods toward the adjoining cornfield.

The players drop their bags and dash for the corn. Jud picks a can off a nail in a tree and gives it to Mule, who goes to the brook to fill it with water.

Cool begins boiling the corn, and the hoboes, who are finished, sit back against some tree trunks and watch. One softly plays "Red River Valley" on a harmonica. They hear clubs banging on freight car doors.

MULE

"What's that?"

"Dicks."

"Dicks?"

"Railroad dicks – copies! Christ, don't he know nothin'?"

SKINNY

"They're comin' this way."

"Aw, they won't bother us. They just want to get everybody out of the cars."

Suddenly a flashlight beam hits Cool's face, and a police dog snaps at him, snarling. The harmonica stops. Three dicks with rifles and badges step into the clearing, pulling the dog back. The white hoboes quietly edge toward the trees. Cool's hand, holding a spoon, is suspended over the pot.

FIRST DICK

"Whadda you boys think you're doin'?"

JUD

"Eatin'."

The flashlight swings to his face, then back to Cool's.

"Your daddy own this railroad?"

MULE

"No sir."

The dick turns his light on Mule.

"You own this cornfield?"

Mule shakes his head.

"Well, then, what you all doin' cookin' this corn on this railroad property?"

Mule's smile freezes. The dick suddenly fires a blast into the can. The water spurts out in a big hiss as it hits the fire. Cool falls backward and scrambles to his feet. Another shot hits the ground beside him.

All the hoboes, black and white, flee into the dark, splash across the brook, streak through the corn, and hurdle a fence. Cool, who got a late start, flies past them almost in a blurr. They race through backyards and finally drop, panting, in a woods. They lie gasping for a short while.

JUD

(laughing and panting:)"Heh, Busher, you sure can move that big ass."

"Hush up, grandpa, you ain't run that fast since your old lady chased you with a rolling pin!"

BUCK

"I wish we had a clock on Cool here. He might just have broke the world record! He runs faster'n a skunk can bump a stump!"

All laugh again.

MULE

(Mutters to himself): "Man, that man can turn out the light and jump in bed before the room gets dark!"

AN ALLEY IN TOWN

To the sound of "I can't give you anything but love, baby, (that's the only thing I've plenty of, Baby)", the players peer around a corner into the street. Across the alley a rat perches on a garbage can lid, gnawing on an onion.

COOL

"Man, look at that poor rat, a-chewin' and a-cryin'."

BUCK

"Yeah. Anytime you see a rat chew on an onion, you <u>know</u> times are tough!"

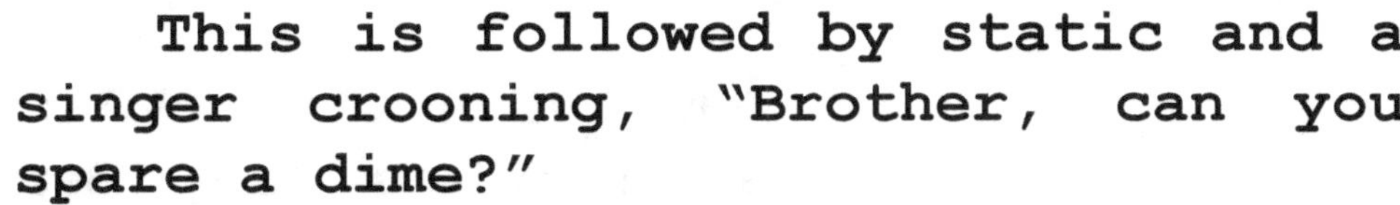

The players stop before a bar hand-written sign in the window, "Free Lunch." From inside comes the sound of a radio comedy show with Jack Benny and his chauffeur, Rochester.

This is followed by static and a singer crooning, "Brother, can you spare a dime?"

JUD

"How much money you got?"

Each one searches his pockets.

SKINNY

"I lost my wallet."

COOL

"I gave Wilkie all my dough for gas, remember?"

MULE

"Me too."

BUCK

"I let Wilkie hold my pay."

Each digs down and brings up a few coins. They put the change in Jud's hand.

JUD

"Thirty-eight cents. Somebody's gotta have twelve more cents." (They shake their heads.) "Busher, you stay here." The others follow Jud inside, where the radio has switched to, "I've got plenty of' nothin'(and nothin's plenty for me)."

They enter a bar.

JUD

"Four draughts."

The bartender sets them up.

BARTENDER

"Forty cents."

Jud pushes the thirty-eight cents toward him. He and the bartender exchange looks. With a half smile, the man shrugs, slides the change off the edge of the bar, throws the bar rag over his shoulder, and saunters away.

The players guzzle thirstily, then rush to the free lunch at the end of the bar. It's a bowl of unappetizing spaghetti and some hard bread. They spoon out big helpings. Cool slips several slices of bread into his coat pocket for Mule.

OUTSIDE A BALL PARK

The stands are empty as Jud, Ben, and Mule come onto the field. Dobie is already there in catching gear.

JUD

(Pointing to home plate:) "Stand there, kid. Ben here is gonna throw you some curves."

BEN

"Just stand there and watch the spin on the ball. It's not gonna hit you."

Ben pitches. Mule instinctively falls away from it. Jud stoops and lays a bat on the ground behind Mule and nods to Ben, who pitches again. Again, Mule falls back, but his spikes land on the bat, and he stumbles onto his butt on the ground.

He gets back up, and they do it again.

DOBIE

"Watch my glove. It ain't gonna move an inch."

The ball heads toward Mule, then curves away into Dobie's mitt.

DOBIE

"See? Easy, huh?"

JUD

"Okay, kid. Now swing."

Ben pitches, Mule swings and sends a line drive over the infield.

JUD

"Busher, I think you got it."

THAT NIGHT

The stands are packed with fans, the blacks in a Jim Crow section in rightfield.

ANNOUNCER

"And now, folks, a special treat. The world's fastest human, winner of four Gold Medals at the Berlin Olympics – Jessie Owens!"

Owens trots out in street clothes, waving.

ANNOUNCER

"And the fastest man in baseball – Cool Papa Bell!

Cool jogs over to home plate and shakes hands with Owens.

The fans set up a chant:

"Race! Race!"

Jesse smiles, shakes his head, and points to his street shoes.

ANNOUNCER:

"Jesse says he'd love to race, but unfortunately he didn't bring his track shoes."

The fans groan.

"But we've got another treat - the Lone Ranger and his wonder horse, Silver!

To The strains of "Flight of the Bumblebee" from the popular "Lone Ranger" radio program, four horsemen gallop through the right field gate into the infield, led by a white stallion, with a masked man waving his white hat and crying, "High yo, Silver, Awaaaay!"

Behind him gallops "Tonto," in buckskin and a feather in his hair, riding bareback on a pinto. Two other cowboys follow on black steeds.

Each rider goes to a different base - the Lone Ranger on third - and they all rein in together as their mounts rear and neigh in unison, while the cowboys wave their hats.

The crowd goes wild.

ANNOUNCER

"Who is faster, man or beast? Are you ready?"

The cowboys wave their hats and halloo as their horses rear and whinny.

Cool takes a sprinter's position at home, next to the first horse. Owens raises a starter's pistol and fires.

They're off. The theme plays loudly as Cool streaks for first beside his four-legged foe. The horse wins by half a length, but Cool hits the bag and flies toward second before the second steed can get started. The horse pounds behind him and catches him, but Cool pushes off the bag one step in front.

The third pinto races in pursuit. The horse is breathing down Cool's neck, but Cool, straining every muscle, turns sharply toward home.

Silver bursts forward with a snort as the Ranger furiously whips the reins from side to side. Cool is straining, the horse is gaining, his mane is streaming, and the fans are screaming.

At home Owens crouches with a stop-watch. Cool slides inside as the horse flies past on the outside.

Owens hesitates. He can't decide. Then he raises his hands high and points to both competitors. It's a tie. he looks at the watch. "Thirteen point one seconds - that ties the major league record!"

Wild cheering from the fans.

Candy: "The rain this morning slowed the track down. His record is twelve seconds, flat."

OWENS

"Man, you ought to be in the Olympics!"

The Ranger circles back, bends down to give Cool a lift up behind him, and together they canter around the stands, waving, in a victory lap.

ANNOUNCER

"And now the star you've all been waiting for - the star of the 1934 World Series - the One, the Only, the world's greatest pitcher - Dizzy Dean!

The great Dean, his brother Daffy, Pepper Martin, and other white stars strut onto the field in their "St Louis Cardinal" jackets. They are the defending World Series champions, and Diz, a good ol' country boy from Miz-sippi, is their biggest star.

Diz greets the Monarchs with affable back slaps and handshakes.

"Hi, Candy.... Howdy, Boojum.... _Como_ _ustar_, Ramon?"

They return the slaps. They have obviously played each other many times before.

Diz nods to Mule, "Who's the new kid?"

CANDY

"Kid, say hello to the great Dizzy Dean... Diz, this here is Mule Samson."

They shake hands.

"This boy is our new secret weapon. He can kick like a Texas mule. Gonna hit more home runs than Jimmie Foxx some day."

"What about Babe Ruth?"

"Yep, maybe more than Ruth."

(Slyly:) "How 'bout Josh Gibson?"

"Maybe more'n Gibson. And who's this new boy the Yankees got? DiMaggio. He'll never hit 'em as hard as my man, Mule."

                              DIZ

"That a fact?"

(Flashing a friendly smile): "Well, I got me a secret, too. See that kid?" He indicates a big blond hefting two bats. "I got him from this college down here. He got a kick like Mississippi corn likker."

                             MULE

"Shoot, if he's so good, what's doing out here? I <u>got</u> to be here. Nowhere else I can go. If he's so good, what's he doing here?

                              DIZ

"You got a pretty chesty kid there, Candy."

                            CANDY

"Wait'll you see him hit, Diz. 'Course, that's if he lives long enough. The way he plays first base, he's gonna get himself killed!"

They all laugh, even Mule.

                          ANNOUNCER

and now - the cardinals' own world famous "Silly Symphony"!

Each Cardinal produces an instrument, mostly home-made - washboard, gut bucket, banjo, kazoo, trombone, etc. Pepper takes out a comb and toilet paper and blows on it to make a "jew's harp." They arrange themselves at home plate for a concert. Dizzy doffs his jacket, revealing a uniform emblazoned "Big League All Stars" on the front, sweeps his cap off, and bows low at the waist in four directions, revealing "the great Dizzy Dean" on the back. With mock gestures he begins to lead his band in a cacophonous chorus of "The Arkansas Traveler" ("once upon a time in Arkansas, an ol' man sat at his little cabin door. . ."

Dizzy doffs his jacket, revealing a uniform emblazoned "Big League All Stars" on the front, sweeps his cap off, and bows low at the waist in four directions, revealing "the great Dizzy Dean" on the back. With mock gestures he begins to lead his band in a cacophonous

chorus of "The Arkansas Traveler" ("once upon a time in Arkansas, an ol' man sat at his little cabin door. . ."

At the end, he takes another series of low bows as Pepper sneaks up behind and kicks him in the rump. Diz whirls and chases Pepper around the bases as the fans laugh and cheer. Pepper slides into home safely just ahead of Diz, who also slides in a cloud of dust as the Cardinals wave their caps and trot off the field.

The Monarchs begin trotting on.

CANDY

"Heh, Buck, you're on first tonight. This boy's momma is gonna be mighty grateful. Mule, you go on out there in leftfield and try not to get hit on the head with the ball."

Mule and Cool jog to the outfield, watched by two kids along the foul line.

FIRST KID

"Heh, look at the niggers. How come your face is so dirty?"

COOL

(Gently): Come on over here, son."

The boys approach haltingly.

"Who taught you to say that?"

They shrug and grin.

"Did your mommy or daddy teach you?"

They shake their heads.

"Did your teacher tell you to say that?"

"Naw. She says to say "colored folk.""

"Then why do you say it?"

"I don't know. It's just easier, I guess."

"Well, all my friends call me Cool Papa. And this is Mule." He tosses them a baseball. "Here. You tell the other kids what I said, okay?"

The boys turn and run off. "Yeah.... Okay.... Thanks a lot."

Practice over, Dizzy and Dobie are talking.

DIZ

"Heh, Candy, ol' buddy, my catcher ain't showed up. How 'bout lettin' Dobie catch me? If he kin hold my high hard one, that is."

DOBIE

"Shoot, I can catch you in a rockin' chair, you big hillbilly."

JUD

"Hell, Candy, then who's gonna catch for <u>us</u>?"

Candy runs out to the Jim Crow section in rightfield and calls to the fans.

"Any of you boys ever done any catchin'?

From the back of the bleachers, Double Duty raises his hand and hustles to the front. He is cherubic and a bit overweight, wearing overalls and clodhopper farm shoes. He clambers over the fence and drops to the ground, where Candy eyes him with amusement.

CANDY

"<u>You</u> can <u>catch</u>?"

"<u>And</u> pitch! That's why they call me Double Duty. And hit like a child of satan, too."

Candy looks him up and down. "Well, you sure can talk okay. "Let's see you catch.

They trot together back to the dugout.

The game begins. Diz takes the mound, Dobie squats behind home. A cop runs out, waving his arms.

"Hold it! Get him off the field!"

Diz meets him halfway to home.

"What's the matter, Captain? Anything wrong?

"You know the law. No nigras and whites can play together. You got to get another catcher.

"Well now, Inspector, if I'm good enough to pitch, he's good enough to catch me."

The cop looks helplessly into the grandstand.

Wilkie rushes over to a white man in fedora in a box seat.

"We've got a week's worth of people here. We gotta play this game."

The man nods to the cop, who shrugs and walks off the field.

"Play ball!"

Cool steps up to bat. "Now," Diz says, "what kind of pitch would you like to miss?"

Dizzy gives a big windmill windup like Paige and unleashes a fastball that whaps into Duty's mitt with a loud crack. Cool swings late as the ump calls a strike.

DOBIE

"Man, Ol Diz is killin' my hands. Get me a bigger mitt, boy!"

The batboy runs to the dugout and returns with a huge padded mitt as the fans laugh and whistle.

ONE FAN

"Get that coon outta there!... Go back to Africa ... Stick one in his old burr-head!"

Cool bunts the next pitch. The ball takes a big bounce in the air as Pepper taps his glove, waiting for it to come down. He whips it to first, but Cool isn't there. He's already standing on second, calmly kicking the dirt off his spikes.

ANNOUNCER

"Do you believe that, folks? A two-base bunt!"

The next batter, Skinny, swings hard, grunts, and hits a weak grounder to first. Buck grunts hard and whiffs.

Diz raises his hat high and waves it as he walks off the mound. The crowd applauds wildly.

Pepper strides toward home, swinging three bats. He discards two and stands in to hit. Duty squats and gives a sign. Bobby nods, pitches, and Pepper drops a bunt and beats it out. Diz points to Duty and yells.

"Heh, new boy! Pepper done stole seven bases in the World Series. If Mickey Cochrane of the Tigers can't stop him, how you gonna stop him?"

Duty smiles and squats, revealing a chest protector with the words, "Thou Shalt Not Steal." Bobby winds up, Pepper streaks for second, and Duty throws to Skinny. Pepper slides, but Skinny blocks the base with his leg, and Pepper is thrown into centerfield. Skinny's pants leg hangs down with a big rip in it but under his torn socks we see a cast iron shin guard and a trickle of blood.

Duty flashes a white smile and rattles the bracelets on his wrist. "You no steal on _me_, boy — you no steal on me."

The next inning Mule walks to bat.

ANNOUNCER

"And now pitching, the hero of the nineteen thirty-two Olympics, with three Gold Medals - Babe Didrikson!"

Babe trots onto the mound, raising her cap to reveal her Dutchboy haircut to thunderous cheers.

Mule pounds the plate. Babe gives a high kick and throws. Mule's eyes pop as the ball whistles over the plate. He tries to swing, too late.

"Strike one!"

The fans buzz with excitement as Mule narrows his eyes, nods, and tenses his jaw. Babe gives him another big motion and kick and delivers, as Mule strides into the pitch - which is a high, slowly arching "blooper pitch." Mule can't stop his swing.

"Strike two!"

Mule recovers and tries to time the descending ball. He starts to swing, stops, starts again, finally lunges off balance and misses.

"Strike three!"

The fans laugh, and Mule trudges back to the dugout, cursing.

Jud pulls a bat from the rack. "She ain't gonna make a fool outta of me!"

CANDY

"Listen, Jud, we're gonna play her tomorrow night too. She draws a big crowd, and that means money in our pockets, so make her look good, okay?"

Jud is cussing under his breath as he steps into the box. Babe throws a curve.

"Strike!"

Jud whirls and shouts."&@%$#! That was a foot outside!"

He squeezes the bat and pounds the plate. Babe throws a fastball, high, and Jud tomahawks it straight back toward her head. She gloves it in self-defense for the out and holds the ball up triumphantly with a big smile as the crowd whistles.

Fifth inning. The Deans lead 2-1. Cool is on first as Mule comes up.

WHITE FAN

"Heh, black boy! Bye-bye!"

Mule hits a whistling line drive against the leftfield fence and lumbers into second.

FAN

"Man, look at that Mexican <u>hit</u>!"

The Monarchs jump up and down. "Kick, Mule!... Way to kick it, boy!... The Mule kicked that one, didn't he?"

ANNOUNCER

"It's two-to-two in the ninth, folks, Cool Papa Bell is up. Mike Ryba of the Cardinals comes in to pitch."

Cool bunts and streaks across first. Mule steps up to bat as Ryba turns and waves his outfielder back. He backs up two steps. The pitcher waves him back deeper. He backs up a couple more steps. At last Ryba turns his attention to Mule, who blasts a long one to deepest center as the fans erupt. Bell streaks for second. The centerfielder races back.

Cool Papa puts on the brakes and hustles back to first. He takes the position of a sprinter in the starting blocks as the fielder leaps, crashes into the fence, and bounces back. The crowd suddenly falls silent: Did he catch the ball or not? Cool raises his glove, with the ball safely in it, and the crowd goes crazy again.

While the fielder picks himself up, Cool is already flying toward second.

ANNOUNCER

(Yelling:) "There he goes!"

CARDINAL PLAYERS

(Screaming:) "Throw it! Throw it!"

The shortstop runs out to take the throw. Cool streaks around second, tearing full-speed for third. In the coaching box Candy is jumping up and down and waving his arms madly. "Go! Go!"

At third base Pepper shouts: "Home! Home!" The throw goes home. Cool slides.

ANNOUNCER

"Did I see what I think I saw? Did he score from first on a fly ball?"

UMP

"Yer out!"

"Out?!"

"Yeah, out! You don't do that against big leaguers!"

Both teams converge on the ump, hollering and waving. Jud and the arbiter shout face to face. Jud slams a bucket over the ump's head and hits it with a bat.

The ump staggers, wobbles, and pulls the bucket off.

UMP

"You're outta here!" He punches his fist toward the bench. Skinny reaches around and socks the umpire from behind Jud's back.

A general melee breaks out. Amid the shoving and shouting, Mule can be seen with a strangle hold on one of the Cardinals. Candy and Diz try to break his grip, but he shoulders them away.

Pepper swings at Bobby, then looks at his knuckles, which have black shoe polish on them. He does a double-take.

Cops charge onto the field with clubs, and two players pin Jud's arms as he takes a blow across the face. A black police van pulls up, and three cops push Jud inside, still screaming.

JUD

"Where's that runt, Skinny? I'll get that midget for this."

The players dust themselves and stick their shirt tails back in. There are apparently no hard feelings. Mule is grinning as if to say, "That was a lot of fun!" Diz picks up Bobby's hat, slaps the dust off it, and hands it to him. Some polish has been rubbed off Bob's cheek. Dizzy squints at him.

The fight breaks up, the players dust themselves off, slap their caps against their knees, shake hands all around, and walk off arm in arm.

DIZ

"You got a big league arm, boy, just like Ol' Diz. Better take care of it. Don't go gettin' in no fights."

Mule walks past.

"Nice hit, kid!"

Mule smiles shyly. Diz takes off his Cardinal jacket and drapes it over Mule's shoulders. "Here ya are, kid. From one champeen to another."

As fans and players file out, Duty and Candy pose with a fan. Wilkie sidles up to Duty.

"Nice game, kid. Want a job?"

The sheriff steps between them.

"No, you don't. This is our boy. He plays for us. We got money bet on him, and you ain't takin' him nowhere. When you leave town, I don't want to see this boy on that bus, hear?"

COLORED ROOMING HOUSE

In a small colored rooming house, the landlady leads the Monarchs down the narrow hallway along a creaking floor.

LANDLADY

"Boys, I only got one tub, and I only fill it one time. Hot water costs money." She turns and strides away.

The players jostle for a spot at the head of the line. The rookies, Bobby and Mule, are at the end. Just then Jud walks in, his head swathed in bandages.

JUD

"Where's that midget? I'll kill the little bastard, so help me!"

Ramon and Candy edge protectively in front of Skinny. Jud pushes past them to the head of the line and sinks blissfully into the tub.

When Jud emerges from the bathroom, Ramon and Ben rush for the door, getting stuck in the entrance.

JUD

"Where's the kid at? The kid goes next!

The players obediently stand back as Jud roughly beckons to Mule at the end of the line.

Later Cool and Mule wearily sit on their bed. Suddenly Mule jumps up. The bed is crawling with bedbugs. With a cry, he furiously stamps on several bugs on the floor. Cool patiently sweeps them off the bed, pulls off the sheets and shakes them out. He takes some newspapers, lays them on the mattress, and smiles wanly at Mule.

COOL

"You'll get used to it, kid. If you leave the light on, they won't come out." He lies down and turns toward the wall. Mule gingerly gets in next to him.

In another room Skinny is in bed when Jud walks in. Skinny springs out.

JUD

"Don't you <u>ever</u> pull that again, ya little midget, I'll kill ya."

Skinny pulls a revolver from under the pillow. "You lay a hand on me, I'll blow your damn head off!"

Jud digs in his bedroll and pulls out a knife. "Yeah? Well, you better not miss!"

He slips the knife under his pillow and lies down. Skinny puts his gun in his shorts and slowly lies down too. They lie there, back to back, Skinny's eyes alert, staring and darting at every little sound as Jud shifts in bed.

HONKY TONK DANCE HALL

Hubbub and loud music - "The Music Goes Round Round, and it comes out here" - fills the room, and dancers fill the floor as Duty and Dobie sit at the bar with their girls. Then they weave through the crowded room.

Duty and his girl walk one way, Dobie and his, the other. Dobie is unsteady as he holds his girl with an arm around her waist.

At her home, Dobie paws her and tries for a kiss. Suddenly angry, she pounds his chest, breaks away, slips in the door and locks it. He beats it with his fists.

DOBIE

"Open up. I won't hurt ya. Lemme in. Come on."

GIRL

"Go away, ya big drunk!"

He staggers around to the back door and gives it a hard shake.

Get outta here! I got a gun. I'll blow your fat brains out."

The lock gives, and Dobie rips the door open. Two loud shots. He cries out, clutches his knee, and stumbles backward down the steps.

NEXT MORNING.

The men stand in front of a movie house showing Errol Flynn in "The Change of the Light Brigade" as Wilkinson and Candy approach.

WILKIE

"I just left the hospital. He's gonna live, but the doctor says he'll never play again."

BUCK

"What's gonna happen to him? He can't do anything else. He don't have any family to take care of him."

Wilkie shakes his head. "I don't know. I left him ten dollars. That's all I got after buying another car, plus eating money for everyone 'til we get to Dallas. If we got any money left after this trip, I'll see if I can pay the doctor. Maybe I can get him a job driving a cab. These are rough times."

The players murmur and reach into their pockets. They come up with a dollar here, some coins there, and hand them to Wilkie.

WILKIE

"Thanks, fellas. I'll mail it to him."

BUCK

"Who you gonna get to replace him?"

Wilkie smiles and winks.

Meanwhile, the Cardinals come out of a white restaurant, picking their teeth. Diz, Daffy, and Bobby come out together.

DIZ

"Mule!"

Mule leaves the others and walks over.

DIZ

"Bobby, where'd you get this big Mule from? If you'n Mule played with me 'n my brother, Daffy, on the Cardinals, we'd win the pennant by July Fourth and go fishin' the rest o' the year.

"Why don't you two ride with me to Dallas?" He opens the car door and tosses Mule the keys.

DIZ

"You better drive, it'll keep those Okie cops off our ass. They'll think you're my chauffeur."

Diz guffaws, but Bobby, who is halfway in the car, leaps back out.

"If he's driving, I'm walking!"

Laughing, Dizzy takes the keys back and hands them to Daffy.

As their car drives away, the Monarchs' bus also pulls out. On the street corner in front of the hardware store, the sheriff sits, tilted back on a chair, a rifle cradled on his lap. He eyes the bus as Wilkie gives him a friendly wave.

"'Morning, Sheriff."

Under the bus Duty is hanging on for dear life, wincing and cussing as the bus hits each pothole.

THE HIGHWAY

Dizzy is driving. Bobby sits beside him, Daffy and Mule doze in the back seat. They stop at a railroad crossing as a train whistles past. Dizzy takes a pull on a liquor bottle while black smoke engulfs the car.

DIZ

"Yeeow! Heh, Daffy, you take a swig o' this white lightnin' yet?"

DAFFY

(Choking from the soot): "No, Diz, I ain't."

"Well, don't. I did, and I've gone plumb blind!"

The train passes, and Diz resumes driving.
                         DIZ
"Where ya from, Bobby?"
"Iowa. I started pitching at a circle on the barn door."
"Me too. I coulda throwed it <u>through</u> the door - if I coulda hit the door!"
He laughs at his own joke.
"How 'bout you, Mule?"
"Scranton."
"You go to school?
"I quit in the seventh grade. Had to go to work."
"Oh yeah? <u>I</u> quit in the second grade. Didn't want to pass my ol' man!"
This breaks him up.
"You got real power, kid. What's the furtherest you ever hit a ball?
"Well, I ain't braggin', but -"
"Hell, if you kin <u>do</u> it, it ain't braggin'.
                         DAFFY
"You know Momma told you never say ain't."
"Hell, a lot of folks who don't say ain't, ain't eatin'."
"Diz, you ain't been right since you got hit in the head in the World Series."
"What d'ya mean? Ain't nothin' wrong with my head. I got x-rays and all."
                         BOBBY
"What'd they find, Diz?"
"Nothin'."
Daffy slaps his thigh and guffaws. Diz throws him a quizzical look.
                         BOBBY
"Mule here can hit 'em as far as Jud ever did."
                         MULE
"Don't tell Jud that!"
                         DIZ

"Is that a fact? And <u>you</u> throw purty near as hard as Lefty Grove,and that's sayin' somethin'. Ain't but one man faster'n Lefty Grove."

                              BOBBY

"Who's that, Diz?"

"Me."

"You really think I'm as fast as Grove?"

"Yeah, you just gotta work on your control and you could be in the big leagues now. And, Mule, if you could hit a curve, you'd be as good as Hank Greenberg. How much you makin' now, Bob?"

"About seventy-five a month. If it doesn't rain."

"Seventy-five! How'd you like to make a thousand?"

"Are you kiddin'? I'd pitch every day for a thouand dollars a month."

"Naw, you pitch twice a week and sit on your ass the rest o' the time. And you don't ride a bus, you ride a train. You sleep in a hotel. You eat anything you want, and the club pays for it – anything up to two bucks. I ain't kiddin'. I mean, I'm talkin' *big league*! You come see me in Florida next March. I can fix you up. 'Course, ol' Diz gets his cut of it."

"Heh, Mule! You hear that? How 'bout that?"

   (Without enthusiasm:) "Yeah, Bobby, that's real good."

                              DIZ

"Listen, kid, you'd be worth a thousand too if, you know...

"Yeah. I know."

"Naw, I mean it. I seen Joe Medwick,I seen Mel Ott. They don't hit 'em any harder'n you do.

"You ain't kiddin' me, are you?"

"Hell no. I'm just a ignorant ol' country boy, but I know they gotta open the doors sooner or later."

"Aw, they'll never do that.""You don't know, Mule. They could."

"I'll be dead by then."

BOBBY

"Naw, Mule. Diz could be right. Look at my father. When he was born, they didn't have any airplanes or cars, even electric lights in his house. You don't know."

DIZ

"Sure. There's too many of you to keep you out forever."

"Yeah, that's the trouble."

"What do ya mean?

"There's too many of us. One or two might be OK, but...

BOBBY

"Diz is right, Mule. They can't lock the doors forever."

DIZ

"Yeah. But ya gotta keep workin' so when the door opens, you'll be ready."

BOBBY

"A thousand dollars a month, Mule! Wow! Think of that!"

Mule turns and stares out the window at the wheat fields in the moonlight, his face is reflected in the window as a few drops of rain hit the pane and slowly trickle down.

A TRAIN CHUGS THROUGH COTTON FIELDS

"The Wabash Cannonball" plays as Mule and Buck slump and doze. Someone's stomach rumbles. Buck rouses himself.

"That you or me?"

MULE

"Me. Man, I ain't had anything since those doughnuts yesterday. How long before we get home?"

"Tomorrow sometime."

"Tomorrow! You sure you don't have any money left?"

Buck digs in his pocket. "Just this." He shows Mule a dime and two pennies. "All that rain just killed us. One game in two weeks. We liked to starved to death! Lucky we saved railroad fare home."
                    CONDUCTOR
"Next stop, Wheeling, West Virginia."
                    BUCK
"Heh, I know all the redcaps here. They used to have their own ball team. Come on!"

He stands, peels back a threadbare blanket he's been sitting on and lifts a pair of trousers from the bench. He inspects the crease. Pulling Mule behind him, he hurries to the washroom.

Buck puts on the trousers, then inspects himself in the mirror, slathers his face with soap, unfolds a straight razor, and begins gingerly slashing his whiskers as the train bumps and lurches. He draws blood from a nostril. "Damn!"

He blots the blood, unrolls his shirt sleeves and buttons them. He buttons his collar and tries to smooth the wrinkles out of the shirt. He pats down his hair, tilting his head left and right to be sure it's just perfect. He turns to Mule and helps him button his shirt.

"Man, gotta look good for my friends."

"Heh, tell 'em we ain't eaten since yesterday. Tell 'em we ran outta money in Alabama, but we'll pay 'em back."

The brakes squeal, and the train begins to slow.

At the station the sound track plays "Pennies From Heaven" as Buck emerges, looking tall and erect. He tugs his sleeves down and strides past a poster for "Mutiny on the Bounty" with Clark Gable and stops at a little shoeshine stand in the shade. Dick Lundy sits in a chair beside it.
                    BUCK
(Gently:) "Dick, it's me, Buck."

"Buck! <u>Great</u> to see you, boy."

Dick offers his hand, and Buck shakes it. Mule suddenly realizes that Dick is blind.

BUCK

"Mule, this here is Dick Lundy. They used to call him 'King Richard.' Smoothest shortstop ever played."

"Naw, John Henry Lloyd was."

BUCK

"Dick, meet Mule Samson. He's gonna be the greatest home run hitter in baseball some day."

Dick holds Mule's hand in two of his for a moment. "You got strong hands, boy."His hands travel to Mule's forearms and biceps. "Yep, you're a ballplayer, all right. Where'd you get those muscles?"

"Diggin' coal."

BUCK

"You should have seen Dick play shortstop, Mule. Best hands you ever saw. They called him "the Shovel." And hit? You could hang out the laundry on those 'ropes' he hit."

Another redcap aged about 70, approaches, pushing a luggage cart. Bucks grabs him by the arms. "Heh, Pop! It's me, Buck!"

Pop looks him over closely, then breaks into a smile. Pop is a gentle, quiet-spoken man with a warm-hearted smile for everyone.

"Buck! You looking good, boy. <u>Glad</u> to see ya."

BUCK

"This here's Mule Samson. He'll be a great hitter some day."

POP

"Glad to meet you, son." He shakes Mule's hand warmly.

BUCK

"This here is John Henry Lloyd. You played against Christy Mathewson and Ty Cobb and those white boys down in Cuba, didn't you?"

Pop nods modestly.

"This is the man that invented shin guards. Right, Pop?"

Pop's eyes twinkle at the memory. "Naw, Frank Grant was first. He was playin' in the white leagues about eighteen-eighty-something. They spiked him so much, he had to wear 'em to save his life."

BUCK

"So when did you play Cobb?"

"About nineteen-aught-nine. Ty was a pretty fast man then. And he would sit on the Bench, say, 'I'm coming down, black boy. Watch out.' I say, 'Okay, come on.' [Pop chuckles quietly.] "We had a great catcher, Bruce Petway. Used to throw out runners on his knees. I just put the ball down, waitin' for Ty when he slid in."

DICK

"'Course he didn't know Pop was wearin' them "stilts" under his socks. Had 'em special made out o' cast iron, didn't you? Ty hit those stilts and bounced into center field. Like to broke his leg."

"We caught him three times that game, remember, Dick? The third time he saw the throw had him beat, so he just turned around and trotted back into the dugout!"

They all laugh.

POP

"He say he was never gonna play against coloreds again. And he never did."

Pop grows serious. "Well, maybe it'll be better for you young fellas some day."

DICK

"So how you fellows doing, Buck?"

"Oh, great, Dick. Real great. They really love us out on those prairies. Big crowds everywhere. We played Dizzy Dean four games, beat him two of 'em. Played Satchel and them. Big crowds everywhere."

Mule nudges Buck hard in the ribs.

POP

"That's real great, boys. I'm glad to hear it."

The conductor yells, "'Board!"

BUCK

"Gotta go. We'll see ya. Take it easy."

Quick handshakes all around. Buck quietly puts the dime and pennies in Dick's change box on the ground and trots to the train. Mule casts a look at the last of their money, turns and follows him.

OFFICE OF SAPERSTEIN ENTERPRISES

Mule, Buck, Cool, and Skinny enter. Abe Saperstein, a short man with slicked-back hair and a handkerchief in his breast pocket, rises to greet them. 

ABE

"Howdy, boys, nice of you to come. Have a seat. . . I guess you have an idea why I asked you to come. You know my basketball team, the Harlem Globetrotters. Well, I've been watching you a long time, and I have an idea that you'd be great stars on the basketball court."

He points to a wall map. "It will be a grand tour, from Chicago to Seattle, down to San Diego, over to Atlanta, and home. If you don't have any other jobs lined up this winter, I'd like you to join it. What do you say?"

They look at each other.

COOL

"I don't know, Mister Saperstein. I haven't played basketball since school.

SKINNY

"Me neither."

                         ABE

"Well, I like your moves on the ball field. You're quick, and you're funny. I think you'd be a big hit. I can guarantee you six months work, from right after baseball season until spring training begins."

                        BUCK

"Well, I just got married. I can't leave my wife that long.

"One hundred dollars a month, plus meals. And no rainouts."

"I don't know - "

"And an extra fifty a month for you if you manage the team."

- "why not."

                        MULE

"I don't know anything about basketball, Mister Saperstein."

"Well, I've got something special planned for you. Ever been to California?"

Mule shakes his head.

"Well, then, this is your chance!"

                  THE BUS. NIGHT

The guys loll asleep, mouths open, snoring. A sign says, "Tunnel Ahead." Mule quietly reaches for a paper bag and blows, inflating it. In the middle of the tunnel, he smashes it - POW!!!

Everyone snaps awake: "What the Hell!"... "Son of a bitch!" while Mule tries to keep a straight face but can't help giving himself away.

              SIOUX CITY HIGH SCHOOL

"Stormy weather" is playing on the sound track, and snow whips into their faces as the Trotters struggle through a snow drift and up the steps of the school.

In the gym, the band is finishing up a rendition of "I've got my love to keep me warm."
ANNOUNCER

"Iowa's own Hawkeye Hoopsters!"

A white team trots onto the court as the crowd claps and the band strikes up "I'm from Ioway - Ioway - that's where the tall corn grows."

Cheerleaders leap, high-step, and toss their batons in the air.

ANNOUNCER

"And on this freezin' evenin', the world-famous Harlem *Globe Trotters*!"

The band sounds off with "There'll be a hot time in the old town toni-i-ight!" as the boys bound onto the court, strutting and jiving and each spinning a basketball on a finger. They form a circle and begin a game of "pepper." They razzle-dazzle the crowd with trick passes behind their backs, between their legs, etc.

The game begins. Buck controls the tip-off, and the Trotters move the ball around. Cool dribbles around his defender and between his legs and passes to Piper Davis, who passes to Skinny - but the ball disappears as everyone looks for it. Piper has never let go and still holds it in his long fingers. He then bounce-passes a long, high "alley oop," which Buck leaps to slam dunk as the fans ooh.

Piper draws a foul, takes a bandana out and ties it around his eyes, then sinks the free throw.
ANNOUNCER

"Piper Davis, folks!"

The Hoopsters shoot, Buck takes the rebound and heaves a long pass the length of the court to Goose Tatum under the basket. Goose turns and centers the ball like a football center to Skinny, who holds it for Cool to kick a field goal cleanly into the basket.

Laughter and clapping.

On the next possession, Piper tosses the ball up and slaps a hot tennis serve to Skinny down-court. Skinny returns a neat backhand. Piper tries a cross-court shot, which Skinny lobs over Goose's head into the basket.

The first half ends, and both teams trot off.

ANNOUNCER

"And now, a special treat. The World's Strongest Man — Mule Samson!"

Mule, clad in a Superman suit and cape, jogs onto the court. He carries a baseball bat in one hand and ten silver dollars in the other. He stops at mid-court, where he holds the bat high, then brings it down quickly and breaks it over his knee.

"Anyone want to try it? Mule has ten silver dollars for anyone who can do the same thing."

Piper trots out with another bat. The men in the stands look at each other. Finally one man stands up in his mackinaw and boots and comes out. He gives the bat a mighty blow against his thigh and immediately hops in pain. Mule smiles and shakes his hand, gives him one of the silver dollars, and leads the crowd in a round of applause, as the man limps to his seat.

ANNOUNCER

"Let's give a big hand to Andy Olson, folks."

Mule takes a stance, legs wide apart, arms held rigidly out to his side.

"Mule still has nine dollars to give to anyone who can pull his arms down. You've got five seconds to do it. Volunteers?"

Several hands go up. "Okay, come on up. Mule will take you two at a time."

The first two come up, and each takes one arm. They strain. They grunt. They lift their feet off the ground. The arms don't budge.

The next two try it with the same result.

"Let's hear it for Mule Samson, the World's Stongest Human!"

The second half begins. Buck tips the ball to Skinny, who dribbles the ball 18 inches off the floor: *Rat-tat-tat-tat*. A defender tries to take it away, but Skinny dribbles it just out of his reach. He lies down, supporting his head with one hand, still dribbling with the other. He lifts one leg, dribbles under it, quickly rolls over, and resumes dribbling with the other hand.

The crowd loves it.

Skinny jumps to his feet and passes to Buck under the basket. Buck dribbles and whirls right for a graceful hook shot. His guard follows his move, leaping to block it. But there's no ball. All eyes search for the missing sphere. Buck calmly takes the ball from between his knees and drops it in the undefended basket.

At the final buzzer, the boys disperse into the clapping crowd to sign autographs.

BENEATH SAN FRANCISCO'S GOLDEN GATE

To the tune of "I left my heart in San Francisco," the Globetrotters' bus pulls up and stops.

COOL

"Well, Mule, here you are, where you always wanted to go – California!"

                    BUCK

"Anybody hungry?"

                    EVERYONE

"Yeah, man!"

                    CANDY

"How about some spaghetti?"

                    "Yeah!"

The bus drives along Fisherman's Wharf to a big sign, and all pile out. As they start in the door, a waiter stops them.

"Sorry, folks, we're all filled up."

They look into the dining room with several empty tables.

                    SKINNY

"What you talking about, man?"

"I'm sorry. They're all reserved."

Muttering, the players file out past a white couple in line behind them.

                    WAITER

(to the couple): "This way, please."

                    MULE

"You sure this is California? I didn't take the wrong road and end up Mississippi by mistake?"

                    TEXAS

"Deep in the Heart of Texas" plays in the background.

                    BUCK

"Heh, stop the car, man."

                    COOL

(Startled awake:)"What is it, man?"

"This here's Galveston Texas."

"This is where my granddaddy came from. I want to take me a look. (They pass a sign.) "Hold up here. Let read this."

The car stops, and they emerge stiffly, stretching their arms and legs. Buck goes over to the sign.

(Reading:) "Galveston's first slave market stood on this site in 1836 after Texas' war of independence from Mexico." They look at the slab in silence, then slowly get back in
the bus.

ALABAMA

"Oh, Suzanna" plays in the background. The players doze or reach under their seats for their "lunch boxes" of groceries and begin making sandwiches. Out of the window they watch a highway sign go by:

Welcome to Decatur, Ala.
Pop. 16,092
BUCK

"Heh, you remember ol' Doc, The pitchin' dentist?"

COOL

"Yeah. Had a spitter like Skinny's."

"That's the one. Couldn't break a pane of glass with the fastball. But he had them batters swinging at his damn slow ball like they was drunk."

SKINNY

"Yeah. Pitched a no-hitter against Rube Foster and the Chicago American Giants."

BUCK

"Yep. And fixed teeth after the game." Buck grins broadly and pulls his lip back, pointing to a glistening gold tooth.

"I thought I knocked that out with a foul tip."

"Naw. You knocked it loose, Doc pulled it out. Didn't have no Novocain. When we got back home, he put in this new gold one."

SKINNY

(Inspecting it critically) "Didn't do no good. You're still ugly."

BUCK

"I think he lives here now. Let's go see ol' Doc, see how he's doin'."

The bus turns off the highway and stops for gas at a sign saying "ESSO… 10.9 cents a gallon." Buck puts the nozzle in the tank while the others head for the men's room.

ATTENDANT

"Heh, you can't go in there."

BUCK

"Oh? Okay."

He hangs the nozzle back up and puts his wallet back in his pocket.

The attendant looks quickly around. "Okay. Just don't let anyone see you."

Back in the car they pass National Guard troops with rifles on the street corners. At the courthouse, state troopers with night sticks and hip holsters line the sidewalk around a Confederate general's statue. A crowd has already begun to gather, a police car with a flashing light on top blocks off a side street, where a group of townsmen is forming behind a barricade. The players peer uneasily. Seeing them, the men shake their fists and jeer.

The bus continues to the colored section and parks.

BUCK

"Man, I don't like the looks o' this."

The players alight and find a door marked
 "F. SYKES. DDS."

They climb the stairs and open the door. Doc, a tall, spare man with a white mustache, is poring over

papers with another man, Sam. A framed picture hangs on the wall. Doc looks quizzically at the visitors.
                         BUCK

   "Doc! It's me, Buck. If you don't remember me, you remember this?" He grins and opens his mouth.

   "Buck! Well, I'll be! What you doing down here?"

   "We been out on the road and passing through town and thought we'd say hello."

   "Well, it's sure good to see you. Sam, these are some of my old baseball friends. This is Sam Lacy of the Baltimore *Afro-American*.
                         SAM

   "I saw you all play a couple years ago. Boojum chased the umpire around the bases and all the way to his hotel.
                         COOL

   "Yep, I remember. They fined him ten dollars."
                         DOC

   "You picked the wrong time to visit, boys."
                        SKINNY

   "What's goin' on?"

   "Serious business. Nine colored kids, about 11 to 18, are being tried for raping two white women in a freight train box car in Scottsboro. They almost got lynched.

"News people from all over the country are down here for trial - New York, Washington, Chicago."

                    SAM

"Doc has been putting me up in his home and driving me around town. Goons follow us wherever we go. This is not a healthy town for black folks now."

                    MULE

"Gee, does President Roosevelt know about this?"

                    DOC

"We're on our way to the courthouse now."

                    CANDY

"You? What you gonna do there?"

"I'm testifying."

"Testifyin'? What about?

                    DOC

"You can come listen if you want to."

The players exchange looks. Hesitantly they nod.

They walk through the gauntlet of police.

In the courtroom they stand upstairs in the gallery with other black spectators. Sam goes to the table with a sign, "Negro Press" behind another table marked "White Press." The front seats are taken by white youths. The nine defendants, ranging in age from 11 to 19, sit at the defense table, looking scared, next to their attorney, Ira Greenberg, a bespectacled man in a rumpled suit.

                    JUDGE

"Mister Greenberg, are you ready to call your next witness?"

                    GREENBERG

(In a New York accent:) "Yes, your Honor. Doctor Frank Sykes."

Doc walks past the spectators, waiting for some to put their legs down so he can pass. He is sworn in as the all-white jury regard him impassively.

                    GREENBERG

"State your name and address."

"Doctor Frank Sykes of Decatur. I was born here in 1893. My father owned a funeral parlor and a general store. I left to attend dental school at Howard University in Washington DC. I have a degree as Doctor of Dental Science."

PROSECUTOR

"I object. What has this got to do with this case?"

GREENBERG

"Your honor, all the defendants are Negroes. But there are no Negroes on the jury. We believe this is a violation of their rights to a fair trial. We contend that there are many Negroes in this county, like Doctor Sykes, who are qualified to serve as jurors."

JUDGE

"Yes, I know Doctor Sykes, knew him from a little boy, knew his father. I think he is qualified to testify on this subject. Go ahead."

GREENBERG

"Thank you, your honor. Doctor Sykes, do you know of other Negroes in this county who are qualified by education to serve on a jury before a court of law?"

"Yes sir."

"How many would you say?

"I have made a careful list of Negroes who have graduated from high school or college, who are sober citizens and conduct businesses here and have done so for many years."

There are some jeers from the front row. The judge bangs his gavel.

PROSECUTOR

"Objection. That's impossible. There is no Negro high school in Decatur."

SYKES

"Your Honor, most of the persons attended high school in Birmingham and other cities, which do have high schools for Negroes."

"Objection over-ruled."

GREENBERG

"Doctor Sykes, how many persons are on your list?"

"Two hundred and sixteen, sir."

GREENBERG

(Holding a sheaf of papers aloft: "Is this the list you compiled?

"Yes, sir."

"Thank you. No further questions."

Doc stands and walks back to his seat. One man, with his foot in the aisle, refuses to move it. Doc steps around it without breaking stride.

It is getting dark as Doc, Sam, and the players walk back to Doc's office. They stop at a cafe.

DOC

"Hungry? This place has the best southern cookin' you've ever tasted. Why don't boys have supper? Sam and I'll make sure my wife and kids are okay. When you're ready just drive a mile down this road; I live in the white house on the right. You all come in and we'll have some ice cream."

NIGHT

The players emerge, pile into their car. and pull out. Across the street another car pulls out behind them. On the highway it turns on its lights.

Mule is driving. The car behind flashes its bright lights, honks, and tail-gates. Mule is blinded. He tries to pull over and let the other car pass, but it stays right on Mule's bumper, still blasting its horn.

COOL

"That must be Doc's house there."

They see a cross burning in the front yard. On the porch two young kids cling to Doc, Sam, and a woman. Doc waves to them to keep going.

                                    CANDY
"Let's get out of here!"

Mule guns the motor. The other car stays right behind, its horn blaring. The two race, almost as one car. Shots whiz past.

When the second car tries to pass, Mule wrenches the wheel to the left to prevent it. A US Highway sign with an arrow to the right flashes past them. Mule jams on the brake and turns on a dime with a loud screech. The car teeters on two wheels, side-swipes the stop sign, and Mule guns the gas again.

The other car misses the turn, hits its brake, and backs up but decides to give up the pursuit. Shot gun blasts are fired as the players' tail-lights recede rapidly down the road.

PART III

1939

CRAWFORD BAR, PITSBURGH

Ella Fitzgerald stands at a mike beside the piano, just finishing her song: "A Tisket, a tasket,(a little yellow basket)." She ends to applause.

MASTER OF CEREMONIES

"Ella Fitzgerald, ladies gentlemen!"

She strolls over to a table and plants a kiss on the cheek of the owner, Gus Grenlee, who sits with a fighter, John Henry Lewis, and several girls. Gus flashes several rings on each hand and clenches a cigar at a jaunty angle between his teeth.

He is a big-time wheeler-dealer with his hands in several questionable enterprises. In the 1920s he smuggled bootleg whiskey when that was illegal. Now he runs a big "numbers" racket, collecting pennies from bettors and paying off up to $500 if their three-digit number comes up (the real odds are 1,000-to-one). It's against the law, but Greenlee pays City Hall to look the other way. Gus may be illegal, but he's not dishonest; he pays the winners scrupulously. He also owns a stable of boxers, as well as the Pittsburgh Crawfords team.

Gus recognizes Mule and Clara in the crowd and calls them to his table.

"Heh, big boy - Mule!"

They take seats across the table. Gus gives Clara a peck and introduces everyone. He wags his finger playfully.

GUS

"That was a helluva ball you hit off my man, Satch, the other day."

Mule grins.

"Satch didn't like that. No, he didn't."

Mule shrugs modestly.

"You know John Henry Lewis, the light-heavyweight champ?"

The two shake hands.

"He's gonna be the next heavyweight champ, aren't ya, big man? I got him a match with Joe Louis in two months. Heh, champ, show us your muscle."

Lewis rolls up his sleeve and makes his biceps dance. The girls touch the muscle and ooh and ah.

                    MULE

"Pretty good, champ."

                    GUS

"<u>Pretty</u> good? Let's see what you got up <u>your</u> sleeve."

Mule shakes his head and gives a little wave of his hand.

                    ELLA

"Come on, let's see."

Mule still shakes his head.

                    GUS

"Want to make twenty easy ones? I got twenty says John Henry can put your arm down on the table in ten seconds."

Gus reaches into his suit, pulls out a wad, and peels off a twenty. Mule looks at it and slowly unbuttons his sleeve. The two men clasp hands, elbows on the table. Gus consults his expensive watch as customers crowd around.

"Go!"

The gladiators strain. Mule's arm slowly bends backward.

Six seconds, seven seconds.... Mule's arm slowly straightens back up... 10.. 11... 12.

Gus slaps the table. He pushes the bill toward Mule, who exhales heavily.

GUS

"Nobody ever did that before. What you doing this winter?"

Mule shrugs.

"How'd you like to make ten bucks a day?"

"Fightin'? No thanks. You got too many fighters already. Most of 'em ain't winnin', but they're all eatin'. How you gonna pay your fighters and your ball players at the same time?"

Gus sweeps his arm around the room. "You ever put a nickel in a juke box in Pittsburgh? You know who owns that juke box? You ever put a penny on a number? You know who gets that penny?" (Gus takes a drag on his cigar.)

"As soon as you play your last game this season, come see me."

At the mike Ella begins her next set: "So let them begin the Beguine..."

PITTSBURGH STREET CORNER

Mule and Shorty walk into view. Shorty indicates a chair beside a doorway. "You just sit here. If anyone suspicious comes around, see this button? You push it."

MULE

What you mean, "suspicious"?

SHORTY

"Like a cop or a detective."

"I push the button? That's it?"

"That's it."

Mule assumes his seat. While he sits, tilted back, two cars pull up, and men get out, carrying sacks of coins. They hurry into the building.

UPSTAIRS ROOM

Men in open vests sit at a long table. They dump the coins out and begin sorting them. Another man puts rolls of coins into a sack for the bank. A third man carries it downstairs.

Time passes. Mule gets up, stretches, and saunters away.

CRAWFORD BAR

A singer croons, "It don't mean a thing (if it ain't got that swing)." Mule enters and goes to Gus' table. Gus holds out a hand.

GUS

"How ya doing, big man? Want a drink?"

Mule shakes his head.

"Could you use a hundred?"

Mule nods. Gus leans forward.

"You know my friends lost the election, and Sunnyman Jackson of the Homestead Grays and his boys are muscling in on my business. The new DA will close me down if I don't give Sunnyman a little 'present.' So all you gotta do is deliver a package for me."

MULE

(Wary:) "Yeah?"

"You know the Homestead Bridge? The little shack on the Homestead side? You just take a box and leave it in front of the shack. That's all."

"When you want me to take this 'box?'"

"Saturday. Two o'clock - A.M. Don't worry, you'll be safe, I promise. Just leave the box. Then you can go home to that gal of yours and sleep like a baby."

Mule sits quietly, thinking it over.

HOMESTEAD BRIDGE - NIGHT

From a nearby bar, drift the notes of "Smoke gets in your eyes." At the far end of the bridge, a single streetlight illuminates the shack. On the near side, a car silently pulls up and stops.

Inside the car Mule and Clara look nervously at each other. Mule peers across the bridge; everything seems quiet. He looks at his wristwatch. They wait in silence some more. Mule checks his watch again, takes a deep breath, and gets out, quietly shutting the door behind him. He begins walking across the bridge.

In the bushes beside the shack, three men crouch, watching Mule come toward them.

Inside the shack, lit by the streetlight, six policemen with tommy guns and revolvers are also watching Mule.

He crosses the bridge and reaches the shack, looking nervously around. He pulls a package from his jacket and carefully places it on the doorstep, then turns and begins deliberately walking away.

When he reaches the halfway point, the men in the bushes behind him creep out. Suddenly, Mule hears the crackling of gunshots and breaks into a sprint.

The police pour out of the shack, guns blazing in the night. Shouts, confusion. The men in the bushes turn and run. Mule hits the ground, then scrambles up and runs across the bridge. He throws himself in the car and slams the door as Clara throws the car into gear and guns it.

ANOTHER STREET - NIGHT

Mule walks alone under a streetlight as a saxophone plays "Mood Indigo." A long limousine follows him slowly. He notices it and walks faster. The car also increases speed. Mule breaks into a trot, then a run. The car pulls ahead of him and makes a sharp turn onto the sidewalk in front of him. Pascual, wearing an overcoat and fedora, opens the door.

PASCUAL

"_Senor_! Just a minute. We want to talk to you."

Mule stops. He looks around for an escape, then enters the car. The door closes, and the car pulls away.

HOTEL ROOM

Pascual and another man open a suitcase full of dollar bills on the bed in front of Mule.

                    MULE

(Whistling) "How - how much is that?"

"Thirty thousand dollars, Amigo."

"Just to play baseball in where? Santa Dominga?"

"Si! Satchel Paige and Martin Dihigo already agreed. You get six more players, you pay them, everything left, you keep. We would like Cool Papa, Jud Wilson - how do you say? - "Double Duty"? -and three more. It's good deal. Santo Domingo nice place, very warm. You like it. Si."

Mule is speechless. He reaches out to feel the bills, unbelieving.

                NEW YORK SUBWAY ENTRANCE

A bitter, windy winter day. The sound track plays "I've got my love to keep me warm." Ramon, Skinny, Cool, Mule, Buck, Benny, and Skinny shiver on the street. Skinny, coatless, hunches his shoulders and coughs. The others huddle in light coats, pull their collars up, blow on their fingers, and stamp their feet. Carpetbag satchels and cardboard suitcases lie at their feet.

                    BEN

"Man! Santa Dominga must be the richest country in the world. You live down south, play two days a week" -

                    COOL

- "Go swimmin', eat coconuts" -

                    SKINNY

- "Drink beer" -

                    BEN

"- Senoritas." He outlines one with his hands.

                    BUCK

"Where the heck's Duty? We can't wait much longer. That boat ain't gonna wait."

He nods toward Slim, a young beanpole of about 20.

COOL

"Well, you don't care, do you, kid? If Duty don't come, you go with us."

Slim shoves his hands deeper into his pockets.

RAMON

"No money, boy? No job?"

Slim pulls his sweater tighter around his shoulder. They wait in silence.

BUCK

"Okay, let's go."

Slim breaks into a smile and reaches for his satchel. They start into the subway entrance when Duty and a girlfriend run up, puffing.

DUTY

"'Bye, Babe. See ya in the spring." He gives her a quick kiss.

SKINNY

"Too bad, kid."
Slim watches the others hurry down the steps, slowly turns, and hunches into the wind.

A SANTO DOMINGO STREET

From a café comes the music of "Chiquita Banana." The players walk on a crowded sidewalk among shirt-sleeved people and soldiers packing guns. They ogle the girls, and the girls ogle back. They pass a movie marquee.

COOL

"Who's this guy, 'Hoy?' He must be pretty good. He's playing all over town."

Duty pulls a postcard from his pocket and drops it into a receptacle marked "BASURA."

RAMON

"Who that for?"

DUTY

"That's my sugar report."

"She no get that long time, friend. That for trash, mon."

Duty darts back to the receptacle, puts his head inside and searches for the card, as the guys all laugh.

COOL

(Nodding to a poster:)"Who's Tru-jill-o? There's more Tru-jill-o pictures than we got Clark Gable pictures back home."

RAMON

"He boss-man, amigo. He say, 'Jump,' everybody say, 'How high?' He say, 'Okay, come down,' everybody say, 'When?' He say, 'Win,' everybody say, 'Yes, boss.' If you no win" - he pantomimes a throat-cutting - "Adios! Comprende?"

BALLPARK

A band in the stands plays "Marie Elena (you're the answer to my prayer)." Latin fans roar a welcome as the boys take the field wearing uniforms of the "Estrellas." Armed soldiers stand impassively among the fans.

El Presidente Trujillo, heavy with medals and epaulettes, sits behind sunglasses in his box, surrounded by be-medaled aides.

Mule steps up to bat. The pitcher, Acosta, gives a windmill windup, kicks, and delivers. Mule swings. Fans high behind home plate watch the ball climb into the sky toward deepest centerfield. The fielder turns and starts to run, then stops and cranes his neck watching the ball fly overhead.

The ball whacks a church about 300 feet beyond the fence and rebounds into a marketplace, causing great consternation.

The people in the stands all shout excitedly and point.

Trujillo turns and snaps an order to a colonel at his side. The officer hands him a pair of field glasses, and he hastily peers into them. He gives another command to a major, who salutes and hurries out of the stadium. He returns with a salute and a tape measure.

Two soldiers dash to home plate. One holds one end of the tape, the other jogs toward the fence and notes the distance. They scramble over the fence and repeat the drill until the tape reaches the church door. While the vendors crowd around, one soldier jots down a number and double-times back to the presidential box. He clicks his heels, salutes, and hands the paper to Trujillo. An aide calls up to the announcer's booth.

ANNOUNCER

(In Spanish, with subtitles): "Ladies and gentlemen. Our esteemed leader, el Presidente, wishes to inform you that the
home run has been officially measured at five hundred and ninety-eight feet."

The crowd gasps. In the dugout Acosta is still shell-shocked.

(Mumbling:) "*Mon*, I <u>never</u> see a ball hit so hard in my life ...."

COOL

"We know that, Acosta. We can <u>see</u> that. But what did <u>you</u> <u>throw</u> him?

ACOSTA

"Mon, I <u>never</u> see a ball hit so hard in my life...."

Next day the players throw the ball on the sidelines while a white pitcher warms up for the other team.

COOL

"Who's that guy?"

BENNY

"Johnny Allen. Going to the Yankees next year."

Jud walks around behind him and watches him pitch.

"That all you got, boy? I think I'll just hold you back a year."

Allen whirls, makes a fist, and the two stare at each other, lips pursed.

The game begins. Jud is at bat. Allen uncorks a pitch at Jud's head. It hits the top of his cap and skips back to the backstop. Jud pretends it doesn't hurt, refuses to rub his head, trots down to first base.

Next at bat, Jud picks up four bats and swings them around his head.

"Watch me get this bastard."

He aims a drive straight back at Allen, who tries to jump aside but the ball hits him in the rear. The two players charge each other and begin throwing punches, rolling in the grass.

Players swarm onto the field. Mule gets a hammerlock on one man, sees the shadow of another coming up behind him, grabs the first by the heels and swings him, knocking both out.

Fans leap over the grandstand wall and join in. Soldiers rush to break it up, and the field is a mass of brawling humanity.

One fan with a <u>machete</u> is at the railing about to jump into the fray. Jud spies him, grabs him by his collar, yanks him over the rail, and pummels him.

A policeman dashes over, unpins a medal from his own tunic and pins it onto Jud's uniform with a salute.

"Muy bravo, Jorocon!"

Jud grins and sallies back into the battle.

Peace is restored. Jud turns to Ramon.

JUD

"What's a "jorocon?"

RAMON

(Puffing out his chest:)"Big Bull!" He laughs.

The game resumes. The batter hits a high foul to left. Skinny chases it as it rolls to the foot of the fence and stops by a pipe. He grabs for it. The pipe suddenly moves, and a snake rears its head and strikes.

Skinny recoils, bug-eyed, runs to pick up a board and returns to beat the snake while the runner races around the bases and the fans cheer and boo.

In the Presidential box, Trujillo turns to an aide and says something. The aide salutes, does an about-face, and hurries away.

Luque, the manager, is angry. He is a big man, who was once a star pitcher in the U.S. major leagues. He is also famous for his temper. Luque screams at Skinny in Spanish as he comes in. Skinny replies with a string of profanity. They stand inches apart shouting at each other, Skinny's neck craned back, Luque's head bent down.

Jud steps between them, his lips pursed. Luque and Jud stare. When Jud finally sits down, Ramon slides over next to him on the Bench.

(His voice low:) "Careful, amigo. The big man (he indicates Trujillo's box), no like that. Just take it easy, okay? If you no do what Luque say, he gonna shoot somebody."

THE CLUBHOUSE

The players are undressing. A radio plays "Flying down to Rio." Joe Cambria, a scout for the Washington Senators, saunters in, slaps some men on the back, punches others on the arm. He feels Mule's muscles.

"Wow, beeg one, right, my friend? Oh, I like see you in Boston! Maybe seventy-five home runs, no? You <u>kill</u> those pitchers back home!"

                    MULE

"Get out of here, Joe. Don't jive me, man."

Cambria stops in front of Cool.

"Ah, human bullet! Oh, I put you in Olympics, boy. Jesse Owens never catch you - on a <u>horse</u>! How many bases can you steal for my team, Washington? I bet a hundred, Easy, easy."

He spies Jud and hunches over like a gorilla, playfully grappling with him.

                  CAMBRIA

"Hah, old man! My <u>papa</u> see you when I was boy. "Oh," he say, "<u>Esse hombre!</u>" - "That man" - he's Big Bull!" My Papa <u>love</u> you."

They wrestle some more. Jud throws him into the arms of Ramon, and the two jabber in Spanish.

                  CAMBRIA

"This man, Cuban <u>maestro</u> - <u>el Diamante Negro</u> - "Black Diamond." When he go in restaurant in Habana, everybody stand up. That's true! You know your manager, Adolfo Luque? Pitch for Cincinnati? Win twenty-seven games one year? He say, "I not greatest player in Cuba - Bragana is!" True, <u>amigo</u>?"

Cambria comes to ROBERTO, a white player with the <u>Estrellas</u>.

                  CAMBRIA

"This boy, Estalella, gonna help us in Washington. Big. Good arm. We lose too many men, army. We need this boy. You be star."

                    JUD

(Muttering to Cool:) "The white leagues even got a one-arm guy. The only thing a one-arm white man can do better than a two-arm colored man is scratch the side that itches."

The door to the manager's office opens, and Luque strides out as all talk stops.

"Heh, you, Wilson, <u>Ven</u> – Come here!"

Jud doesn't move.

"<u>VEN</u>!"

Jud slowly walks toward the office. The door closes. Their muffled voices come through the partition. The players are quiet for a few seconds.

Cambria spots Skinny across the room.

CAMBRIA

"Heh, Skinny! Look this arm. You no got arm, you got a cannon! Good double-play man. Oh, we need you in Washington, too. How about you learn the <u>lingo</u>? We say you <u>Cubano</u>."

Skinny shakes his head.

CAMBRIA

"Heh, Ramon! You teach this man Spanish, okay?"

Skinny shakes his head again.

COOL

"Why not, Skinny? You can do it."

SKINNY

"Nah. Thanks, but – "

MULE

"This is your chance, man. Go get it!"

SKINNY

(Suddenly angry:) "You guys crazy? Maybe if I was younger...."

DUTY

"Who they got in the white leagues better than you? Phil Rizzuto? Pee Wee Reese?"

"Yeah, but everybody knows me. I'd never get away with it. And you know it! So leave me alone, for Chrissake!"

The voices through the partition suddenly grow louder. Sounds of a struggle, bodies banging against furniture. A shot rings out, and the noises stop. The players freeze! They look wildly at each other. Then they rush for the door and shoulder it open.

Jud is holding Luque's head in a death grip. The gun, still smoking, lies at their feet. Mule and Ramon tear Jud away.

BUCK

"Don't <u>do</u> that, man! You scared the hell out of us!"

A CANTINA (BAR)

The boys are sitting around a table, having beers, each with a girl at his side or on his knee. The juke box plays, "Drinking rum and Coca Cola." Mule shares a cigarette with his girl. He seems high.

MULE

"Just one more game. Man, ever get home, I'm <u>never</u> comin' back."

RAMON

"No more beer, or you no <u>get</u> home, <u>amigos</u>. Sleep now."

He pulls Mule's arm, but Mule shakes him away. The door bursts open, and three soldiers with weapons enter.

SOLDIER

"<u>No cerveza</u>! <u>No mas</u>! You, <u>carcel</u>! <u>Vamos</u>!"

Two men grab Mule's arms. He flings them away with a grunt. Ramon jumps between them, pushing Mule back down.

MULE

"I ain't going to no jail!"

RAMON

"You listen! We go. Quiet, man.... Quiet. Okay?. .. Okay?"

He speaks to the soldiers in Spanish.

RAMON

"They say, "Win tomorrow, then drink." (More softly:) Come, okay?... Okay... Good man."

Mule relaxes and rises. The others also get up.

DUTY

"Can she come too?"

SOLDIER

"No talk. Go!"

The soldiers herd them to the door.

JAIL

The soldiers give the boys a push and slam the cell door.

Mule punches the wall.

"What the hell kind of country is this? Just like America! Push you around. What do they think I am? They're all the same, don't matter where I go."

He falls exhausted onto a bunk. The others wearily climb onto theirs.

AN AIRFIELD - NIGHT

The boys peer out through dark shadows beneath palm trees on the edge of the runway. They suddenly crouch as two soldiers walk past on the other side of the tree. On the runway, the propellers of a two-engine plane begin to turn. They stealthily creep closer to the field. Someone farts, and Skinny snickers. Ramon claps a hand over Skinny's mouth.

COOL

(Whispers:) "Man, Jud, you like to got us killed! I'm never coming back here with you again!"

JUD

"You don't shut up, you won't come any place again!"

Ramon motions them down. He cautiously raises his head and looks. The plane is slowly taxiing toward them. He motions them forward.

A Shout is heard and some shots. Duty is running toward them down the runway, closely followed by a man with a <u>machete</u>.

MAN

"You no fool with <u>my</u> wife, you <u>Yanqui</u> bastard!"

Duty races toward the plane and leaps inside as the <u>machete</u> misses him by inches. Thirty yards behind the man, soldiers are running toward them.

RAMON

"Go! Go!"

Mule darts toward the plane, followed by the others, carrying their suitcases. Some suitcases fall open as they run. Two more shots are heard. Someone in the plane holds the door open and waves them on. They pass their satchels inside. Mule pushes Skinny on board and jumps in himself.

Cool runs toward the soldiers, and they swing their guns around to him. Two shots miss. The soldiers pursue Cool, as Ramon and Jud reach the plane, which is picking up speed for takeoff. Cool runs a ring around the soldiers and out-sprints them as the plane passes him. Four arms reach out and grab him as Cool's feet and the plane's wheels leave the ground at the same time.

The plane roars above the trees with Cool still half outside as shots crackle from below. The moonlight reveals Cool's feet slowly disappearing into the plane as it
roars into the night.

PART IV

1941

BARBER SHOP, CHICAGO
Crawford and Monarch players lounge on chairs, waiting their turns, as Mule gets a trim. The radio plays Judy Garland singing, "Somewhere Over the Rainbow."
CRAWFORD PLAYER
"What you say, Big Boy? You gonna hit a homer in the All Star Game tomorrow?
MULE
"I hope so."
"Yeah, but Satchel's pitching. You never kicked one against Ol' Satch, did you?"
"Sure I have. He don't bother me."
"He don't?"
"Naw. I hit him just like anybody else."
The Crawfords exchange smles.

OUTSIDE COMISKEY PARK, CHICAGO
In the background come the strains of "Chicago, Chicago, That Wonderful Town," which segues to "We're Havin' a Heat Wave, a Tropical Heat wave..." Men mop their brows and fan themselves as a crowd files through the turnstiles. A sign proclaims
"1941 EAST-WEST GAME... Biggest Stars of the Negro Leagues... Satchel Paige, Joe
NEWSBOY
"Read all about it! HITLER INVADES RUSSIA! DIMAG STREAK PASSES HORNSBY!"
Charles Comiskey gives the boy a nickel, and takes a paper. The boy starts to pocket the money, but Comiskey waits for change. He turns the paper over to the back-page headline:
SATCH + MULE = FLAG FOR SOX?
Will Baseball
Open Its Doors?
He tucks it under his arm and joins the crowd going into the park.

In the batting cage Mule is hitting long drives, one of which clears the roof as the fans gasp and poke each other.

In his box seat Comiskey almost swallows his cigar. When Mule trots off the field, Comiskey calls him over.

COMISKEY

"You looked pretty good, boy." (Mule smiles.)"You know who I am?"

Mule waits.

"Charles Comiskey. This is my park."

He sweeps the grandstand with his arm.)

"Babe Ruth's the only man ever put one out of here before, back in nineteen twenty-seven. Lou Gehrig couldn't do it. Joe DiMaggio can't do it."

"Yes sir.

"You sure got good shoulders." (Mule beams.)"You going to hit a homer for me today?"

"I'll try, Mister Comiskey."

"Keep up the good work, boy. Good luck to ya."

DRESSING ROOM

The open newspaper lies on a bench with the headline showing as the players lounge before the game.

COOL

"I'll believe it when see it."

JUD

"Same old BS."

MULE

"Aw, they wouldn't joke about a serious thing like this."

Jud sneers.

A white newsman, D'Angelo, enters and extends his hand to Mule.

"Hi. D'Angelo. Daily Worker."

RAMON

(Whispers to Cool:) Daily Worker?

(Whispering:) "He's a Commie."

D'ANGELO

"What do you think, Mule? Think you could make the White Sox?"

JUD

"Huh? Who they got catchin'?"

"Luke Sewell."

"How many homers he hit last year?"

"None."

"What do you think?"

They all guffaw.

D'Angelo pulls a paper from his breast pocket. "Here. This is a petition. We want the commissioner to open the big leagues to you guys."

He pushes the paper and a pen toward the players. Skinny starts to take it.

BUCK

"Wait a minute. We're not signin' anything."

"We'll put it in the paper. They'll have to give you a tryout."

"You can print anything you want. We know we can make the team. But we came here to play ball."

The players file out. Wilkie is left standing in the background.

D'ANGELO

"What do _you_ think, Wilkie? You'd lose most of your team if they open the doors."

WILKINSON

"Yeah. I know."

He follows the players out.

ON THE FIELD

The loud strains of "When the Saints Go "Marching In" erupt, and Louis Armstrong

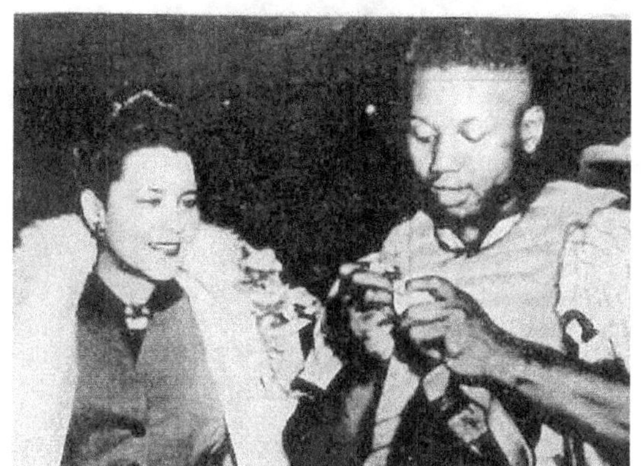

struts out of the stands toward the pitching mound to wild cheering.

Players from both teams boogey out of the dugouts behind him and split into two lines along the base lines for introductions.

Armstrong takes a bow, and Mule and the players peel off to sign autographs (left, Ms Joe Louis, the wife of the heavyweight champ).

Comiskey turns to his aide, Flanigan. "Where's Satchel? The fans are getting restless."

A HOTEL ROOM

Satchel is pitching pennies with two young women, as Chet, his roommate, tugs at his sleeve. Satchel pulls his arm away.

"Man, let me be, Dooflackem. I got serious business here."

"The game starts in thirty minutes, Satch."

Satch takes careful aim and tosses.

"So?"

"So we're fifty miles from the ball park."

"We _are_? Why didn't you _say_ so?" (He rakes in his winnings.) "Bye, gals. See ya next time I'm in town."

They run out of the hotel and leap into a convertible. Satchel wheels the car away from the curb in a big U-turn, narrowly missing an oncoming car, and careens across a pedestrian island, scattering the people as he passes.

COMISKEY PARK

Cannonball Dick Redding glares from the mound as Mule pounds the plate.

In the stands two loud fans in fedora hats and wide lapels flank a pretty girl, Clara.

"Come on, Mule, baby. Kick, Mule!"

"Kick, hell! He ain't even gonna <u>see</u> Cannonball's fast one, man!"

Clara concentrates on Mule.

Josh, the catcher, pounds his glove, holds it for a low pitch:

JOSH

"Come on, Cannonball, baby, bring it here!" Cannonball reaches back and throws over Mule's head into the screen. Mule ducks.

"Man, Cannonball's wild today... Heh, you know that little gal you were out with last year?"

Mule tries to ignore him.

"Well, she's in town. I went out with her last night."

Mule looks back to reply as the ball whooshes over the plate.

"Stee-rike!"

JOSH

"Heh, you know something else?"

Mule grits his teeth and takes two vicious practice swings.

"We didn't get a wink of sleep."

Mule beats the next pitch into the ground off his front foot and hops around, cussing.

"You know what else?"

Mule is really seething now.

"We're gonna do it again tonight!"

Mule flails at the next pitch for strike three.

Next inning Josh takes his turn at bat. The big Indian pitcher, Cyclone Joe Williams, stares in malevolently, and Double Duty squats in the catcher's box.

DUTY

"You nice and comfortable now? Got a good hole dug there? You better stay loose, 'cause you just dug your grave. Joe don't like nobody taking a foothold on him. Man, when he's wild like this, he even scares <u>me</u>!" (He pounds his glove.) "Stick one in his ear, Joe""

Joe takes a big windup, kicks his foot high, and throws. The ball whistles in, high and inside. Josh ducks at the last minute, sprawling on his butt.

"To tell you the truth, I didn't hardly see that one myself. The Indian's fast today, ain't he? But he don't have <u>no</u> control."

Josh connects with the next pitch and sends a long blast into the upper deck in left.

In the press box Ed Burns of the Chicago <u>Tribune</u> is the only white man there. "Wow! Does he do that often?"

Sam Lacy stops typing. "No, only about once a week. You should have been here last week. See that last row in rightfield, over the four hundred-five-foot mark?"

He points with his pipe. "Josh put it there. Line drive, too. I've seen Mule hit it over the roof a couple times."

Burns writes it all down furiously.

Duty comes into the dugout and throws his mask against the wall.

SKINNY

"What you call for, Duty?"

(Angry:) "A fastball."

"Why didn't you call for curve?"

"God Damn! If I'da <u>knowed</u> he was gonna hit the fastball, I <u>woulda</u> called for a curve!

SMALL TOWN STREET

Chet grabs his hat with one hand and the windshield with the other, as the car screeches into a left turn inches ahead of an on-coming car. Next it is weaving in and out among other oncoming cars, who honk in alarm and run up onto the sidewalks.

CHET

"Satch!! This is a one-street!"

SATCH

(Swerving to avoid a lamppost): "You worry too much, Dooflackem. I'm only goin' one way."

A siren sounds behind them.

COMISKEY PARK

A lefty, Luis Tiant Sr, is pitching. Cool walks. Skinny steps up to bat. Jud is coaching at first base.

JUD

"Watch out. This guy's got a great pick-off move. You can't tell if he's gonna throw to first or home."

Tiant sets with his hands at his belt. He steps and throws to first. Cool scurries back. Skinny swings. The crowd laughs.

"Strike one!"

Next pitch. Cool streaks to second

while Tiant is still winding up. Skinny bunts toward third. Cool is already at second and still flying. Tiant and the third baseman converge on the ball, leaving third base open. Josh runs to third to cover the bag. Too late - Cool has already crossed it and is heading toward the now unguarded plate. Tiant wakes up and dashes to the plate, but Cool slides across while all the fielders shout and point at each other.

Skinny slides safely into third.

Burns slaps his forehead in disbelief. "Wow, that's a new one, scoring from first on a bunt! I never saw anyone do _that_ before!"
                    LACY
"Shoot, he does it all the time."

On Mule's next at bat, the fans stand to cheer. He slaps a grounder and trots back to the dugout. The fans slump back in their seats.
                    FAN
"You call that a kick? I got a _chicken_ can kick harder'n that!"

                SMALL TOWN BARBER SHOP
Satch, Chet, and a policeman sit while the barber snips the judge's hair. Chet fidgets, Satch smiles benignly.
                  SATCHEL
"Excuse me, Judge, sir, I got a game I got to pitch in Chicago. Can I pay my fine now?"

The judge looks up from _The Police Gazette,_ a girlie newspaper, and scans Satch's ticket.
                    JUDGE
"Mmmm. Speeding, disobeyin' traffic signs, expired driver's license. That'll be twenty dollars."

Satch reaches for his wallet and counts out four ten-dollar bills. "Here you are, your honor, sir."

"What's this for? I said twenty, not a forty."

"That's Okay, Judge. I'm comin' back tomorrow. (To policeman:) "Come on, Wild Child, we got a game to make!"

They hurry out the door. The players jump in their car, the policeman kicks his motorcycle stand and noisily stands on the pedal. He turns his siren on and leads Satchel's car at top speed out of town.

COMISKEY PARK

A new pitcher, Wild Bill Brown, is on the mound as Josh steps in to bat. Wild Bill turns to the centerfielder and waves him back. The outfielder retreats a few steps. Bill waves him back some more and farther to the left. Then back some more.

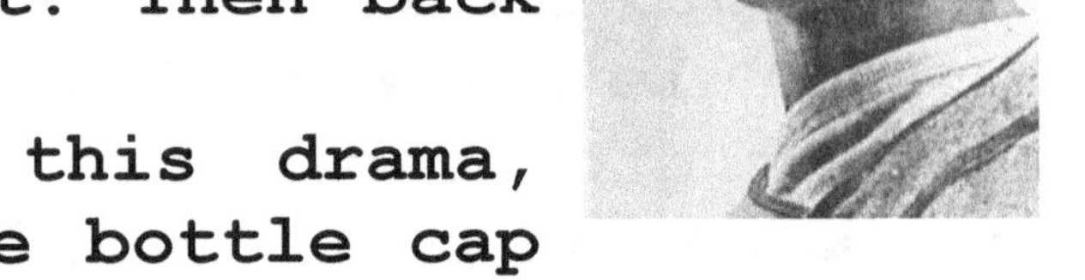

While everyone watches this drama, the third baseman has a Coke bottle cap

in his glove and gives the ball a quick scrape and toses it to the mound.

Josh hits another long, high drive. Mule, in left, doesn't even move. He cranes his head back and watches it. In the upper deck the fans leap to their feet, screaming, as the ball lands among them and they fight each other to catch it. Josh circles the bases with a wave of his hat.

Mule comes up a third time.

ANNOUNCER

"A new pitcher for the East, folks. <u>Cocaina</u> Garcia, "the Cuban Cannonball!"

JOSH

"You know why they call him "<u>Cocaina</u>?" 'Cause he makes the batters all look drunk on cocaine. He's got a million pitches, and they're all in Spanish. You know the <u>lingo</u>? I'll even tell you what he's gonna give you."

He yells to the mound in Spanish.

"Heh, Jose! _Muy rapido, bueno_?"(To Mule:) "That means 'curve.' I hope he understands my <u>lingo</u>, 'cause if he don't, even <u>I</u> don't know what's comin'."

Garcia fires. The ball dances crazily as Mule hesitates, then takes a late swipe and misses.

JOSH

"Wow! That's a new one even I never saw before!"

In the dugout the players leap to their feet, shouting and pointing: "He cut it!... Heh, ump, take a look at that ball!"

The umpire calls for the ball, gives it a quick glance, and throws it back to the pitcher. "Get back up and hit."

Josh yells gibberish to the pitcher. To Mule:

"I don't remember, does that mean curve or fastball? Oh, well, you're not gonna hit it anyhow."

The pitch is over Mule's head into the backstop. Garcia quickly spits into his glove, takes the throw from the catcher, twists it in the glove, winds up, and throws. The pitch comes in high, Mule takes a mighty swing, and the ball suddenly darts low. The ump cocks his finger like a pistol and "shoots" Mule.

"Stee-rike."

Mule wipes his eyes. "Heh, man, how you see that ball with all that spit flyin' in your eyes?"

JOSH

"What's the matter? <u>I</u> see it. Everybody here sees it. How come <u>you</u> can't see it?"

The next pitch wobbles and darts, and Mule hits a foul. He pounds the bat into the ground as Josh laughs.

At last Mule swings and sends a long drive to left. Clara jumps to her feet with the other fans.

The leftfielder backs against the wall, leaps, and one-hands it for the out.

OUTSIDE THE STADIUM

Behind the howling siren, Satch's car roars up to the gate and stops so fast that Chet is thrown into the windshield. Satchel hops out, pulling off his shirt as he hurries through the gate.

BOTTOM OF THE NINTH

The score is 6-6 as Satchel dashes onto the field, still tucking his uniform shirt into his pants. The crowd erupts with cheers and whistles.

"That's it. It's all over now!"

UMPIRE

"No time for warm ups, Satch."

Satchel calmly walks the first batter in four pitches, then makes eight pick-off throws to first base and nods that he's ready. He surveys the next hitter Buck.

JOSH

"Give him the 'Midnight Creeper,' Satch. He'll never hit it."

Paige turns to his fielders and motions for them to sit down. They look at each other and shrug, and one by one, they sit with crossed legs, watching what Satchel is going to do.

The fans are going crazy, and the manager, Duncan, bolts out of the dugout. Josh and all the infielders meet him on the mound. Everyone is waving his arms and talking at once.

DUNCAN

"Are you crazy?! This is no time for clowning. There are fifty thousand people here. We want to win this game!"

"Don't worry, Skip, I'll win it."

Grumbling and shaking their heads, the crowd at the mound at last disperses. The next batter, Skinny, reaches out and taps a ball on the ground. The fielders all laugh, but no one gets up to chase it. Satch huffs and puffs after it and finally flags it down in short right field as the runner slides into third and the batter takes second.

There is mixed hilarity and anguish from the fans. Josh rips off his cap and stomps to the mound.

"Let's give this next guy your 'Four-Day Wonder,' Satch. He won't even see it."

"I'm gonna walk this guy."

"What?!"

"I know what I'm doin'."

Josh shrugs and goes back behind the plate and holds his mitt out for an intentional walk. The fans are abuzz.

BURNS

"What the heck is he doing?" The other writers shrug and shake their heads.

Duncan, the manager, pulls his hair, kicks the water cooler, grabs his toe in pain, and hurries, hopping, to the mound. An agitated crowd forms around Satchel. A bevy of cameramen madly pop flashbulbs. Duncan sputters and waves his arms, but the noise drowns out his words. Above the sea of bobbing heads, Satchel's head can be seen, smiling serenely, trying to calm everyone.

JOSH

"It's his money too, Skip, just like it is ours. Let's see how he does."

Everyone slowly disperses. Duncan stomps back into the dugout with a dark backward glance. He punches the dugout wall and shakes his hand in agony, hopping on one foot and blowing on his hand at the same time.

Satch lobs four pitches, all outside.

FANS

108

"Kick, Mule!..."

"You got him, Satch; he can't hit it if he can't see it!... Goodbye, Mule."

SATCHEL

To Josh: "I done heard what you said about hittin' me just like you hit everyone else. Well, I fixed it so it's just you and me. I ain't gonna trick you now. I'm gonna give you 'bees at the knees.' No 'smoke at the yoke.'"

Mule pounds the plate, Satch slings side-arm, and Mule leans out, expecting a curve. Instead, a fastball sails in, inside, and he has to hop out of the way.

The umpire cocks his pistol.

"Strike!"

Bedlam in the stands.

SATCHEL

"Think I'm fooling you? Here comes another one, same place, only a little bit faster."

FAN

"<u>Kick</u>, Mule!" Clara crosses her fingers and shuts her eyes.

Mule doesn't believe him and moves his front foot closer to the plate, expecting a curve. Satch smiles and throws. Mule pulls his bat back from an inside strike three.

BURNS

Burns: "Son of a bitch! I never saw anything like that in the major leagues!"

Lacy blows a smoke ring. "You mean the <u>white</u> major leagues."

Satch boogies to the East dugout, where the players are glowering, with arms folded.

"Tell <u>that</u> to the boys in the barber shop!"

Bottom of the 12th. The West is leading 7-6. Two out. Big Bill Foster, a lefty, is on the mound. Cool catches him off balance with a bunt single.

MULE

"Skinny, go up there and kneel in the on-deck circle; they'll think you're up next."

Skinny takes his position. Josh sees Skinny, stands up, and holds his glove out for an intentional walk. Jimmy trots to first, Skinny goes back to the Bench, and Mule strides out instead. Josh does a double-take.

ANNOUNCER

"Samson is the East's last hope. He's had a horrible day - no hits in four at bats."

Josh squats, flashes the sign, and pounds his mitt. Foster glares at Mule. Mule glares back.

A fastball comes in low and on the outside. Mule swings with a great grunt and a crack like an explosion. The ball flies into the lower stands, foul.

Next pitch. Mule starts to swing, then pulls his bat back. Strike two!

The crowd erupts. Mule reaches down, scoops up some dirt, and dusts his hands. He gets back into the box. The muscles of his jaw tense. The big stadium is hushed

Foster turns his back, whirls, and pitches. Another mighty grunt, another CRACK that echoes through the stadium.

The centerfielder backtracks to the fence, as the ball goes over his head and into a loudspeaker, rattles around, and drops out. The fielder grabs it and heaves with all his might.

Jimmy slides home to tie the score.

Mule is legging it to third for dear life. The shortstop runs out to take the relay. Josh blocks the plate. In slow motion Mule stumbles rounding third, recovers, and barrels head-first into Josh. A cloud of dust obscures the play, but the thud of their collision can be heard throughout the park.

Freeze frame.

The umpire slowly spreads his palms: Safe.

The players rush out of the dugout to hug Mule.

Clara jumps and shouts.

HOTEL BALLROOM

Duke Ellington's band is playing "Take the A-Train." Buck and his wife jitterbug.

Satch, Cool, Ramon, Skinny, and Duty crowd around Clara.

SATCHEL

"....No, I ain't married, but I'm in great demand!"

Suddenly, the band stops and breaks into "Hail, the Conquering Hero," and a spotlight swirls, then stops on the balcony above the dance floor, where Josh, in a white suit and white shoes, waves and grins broadly. Amid applause, he vaults over the balcony railing to the floor below.

He pushes his way confidently through the crowd to Clara's side.

JOSH

"You're a mighty beautiful lady. How 'bout showing these dudes some <u>real</u> dancing!"

CLARA

"No <u>thank</u> you! Big man like you, going to crush a little woman like me to *death*!"

PLAYERS

"Ol' Josh, he can hit, but he can't score!"

Cool is wearing a zoot suit with a garish jacket of multi-color stripes.

COOL

"Ma'am, I promise: My feet will never touch the floor or your feet."

He offers his arm and leads her onto the floor. Cool looks at Duke, who nods and smiles and strikes up Ellington's "In My Solitude (you haunt me)." Cool begins slowly, then goes into a whirl as her eyes widen, and she follows him perfectly. The other dancers back away, and Cool gives Clara another whirl and ends with a dip so low that her head almost touches the floor.

Duke switches to "Take the A-Train (if you want to get to Harlem in a hurry)". Cool goes into a jitterbug as Clara laughs and waves her free hand. He pulls her toward him and swings her around his shoulders as the watchers clap. The vocalist ends with a flourish, and the dancers end with a split to loud applause.

Then Cool gallantly offers his

arm again and leads her back to the group. He bows, and she curtsies, breathing heavily and touching her brow with a hankie. Smiling radiantly, she turns a Mule.

CLARA

"Mister Samson, would you get me a drink of punch, please?"

Mule looks flustered, but Clara takes his arm and steers him through the crowd toward the punch bowl.

Cool watches them as the band plays Ellington's "I Let a Song Go Out of My Heart."

HOTEL HALLWAY

The sound of the band playing "Roll Out the Barrel(we'll have a barrel of fun)" wafts up from the ballroom. Satchel jives to his room, a lady on his arm. They shut the door behind them.

Downstairs the band has switched to "I'm In the Mood for Love." The door opens quietly and Satchel tiptoes out. He crosses the hall and raps softly on the opposite door.

(Whispering): "Nancy?.... Nancy?"

As the door slowly opens, suddenly the door behind him swings open too, and a woman in bathrobe bursts out.

(Shouting:) "Nancy? _Nancy_!? Who's this Nancy?"

Now a third door opens. Buck sleepily looks out and quickly sizes up the situation.

"Yeah, Satch, what you want?"

ANOTHER ROOM

Downstairs the band is heard lustily playing "ONE O'CLOCK JUMP." Skinny enters, lurching tipsily. Jud is snoring in his bed.

SKINNY

"Okay, ya big baboon! Get up! Let's have a drink!"

He sits down on Jud's bed. Jud turns and mumbles a curse. Skinny gets up and flips the light switch on. Jud growls from under a pillow.

SKINNY

"Up! Up! Ya big hyena! We're gonna party tonight!"

Jud rouses himself and sleepily swings his feet onto the floor. "You little midget. If you Don't shut up, I'll shut ya up!"

Jud grabs one of Skinny's ankles and hoists him upside down into the air. He carries Skinny, kicking, to the window. Holding Skinny with one hand, Jud raises the window with the other and holds Skinny out.

Skinny looks down at the sidewalk six stories below.

"Let me go, you damn madman! Turn me loose!"

The people below look up to see Skinny kicking furiously with his free leg. He lets go of his bottle, which falls to the sidewalk and hits the ground with the loud sound of shattering glass.

Skinny's free foot is still kicking Jud's arm and drawing blood. Jud sleepily switches hands. At last he hauls Skinny in. Now completely sober, Skinny looks bug-eyed out the window to the street below. He turns to walk to his bed, takes one step, and his legs buckle.

A SECOND ROOM

Cool, in pajamas flicks the light off. Nothing happens. He looks quizzical, when the light suddenly goes off. He flicks it back on and tries again. Same thing. Finally, he shrugs and finally gets into bed.

The door opens, and Mule floats in, looking dreamy, his shirt pulled out, tie undone, lipstick all over his collar and face.

COOL

"Sit down, Roomie. I want to show you something." He gets up, walks to the light, flips the switch, then strolls back to bed and pulls the cover up.

Bing! The light goes out.

"See," he says in the dark. "You been tellin' everybody that story 'about me all these years, and even <u>you</u> didn't know it was true!"

HOTEL HALLWAY

The singer is crooning, "I Can't Give You Anything But Love, Baby... (That's the only thing I've plenty of, Baby)." Fingers to their lips, Ramon and Skinny, in their shorts and undershirts, tiptoe to a door and listen to groans and gasping inside.

SKINNY

(Whispers:) "It's Double Duty."

Quietly they pull up a chair to peek over the transom, standing on tiptoes and elbowing each other for a better view. The chair begins to totter. Skinny loses his balance, grabs Ramon, and both fall through the door onto the bed to startled shrieks and curses.

NEXT DAY

Satchel, Josh, Mule, and Cool negotiate the crowds on the street. they pass a movie marquee advertising "Citizen Kane" and enter an office building.

they emerge from an elevator and enter an office door marked

White Sox
Mr Comiskey
President

They enter and stand diffidently at the receptionist's desk. Comiskey comes out with a handshake, clapping them on their backs.

"Hell of a game, boys... Hell of a game." He punches Josh and Mule on their arms. "Where'd you get those muscles, boys? I haven't seen anyone hit like that since the Babe."

He pinches Paige's slim arm. "And, Satch, you don't have any muscle at all! It's all bone. No wonder you never get a sore arm."

He turns to his aide, Ed Flanagan. "You ever seen anything like that, Ed?" Flanagan smiles and shakes his head. The players beam.

COMISKEY

"The newspapers want me to sign you boys to the White Sox. What do you think of that?"

The players look at each and shift weight.

"Well, let me tell you: If we take you boys, it will break up your league."

SATCH

"Well, we don't know anything about that."

JOSH

"We think we could make the team. We think we could help you out."

COMISKEY

(Cocking his head and clicking his tongue.) "I'd give fifty thousand dollars for you" - they beam - "if only you were white."

Their smiles fade. Comiskey claps their shoulders and eases them to the door with a final handshake.

Burns enters as they go out.

BURNS

"You going to sign those boys, Charlie?"

"No, nothing to those rumors."

BURNS

"I've been covering the Cubs and White Sox for over ten years now, and I never saw anything like those guys played. You're in sixth place. You could use some power and more pitching."

"Yeah, they got power. But can they hit a major league curve? And Satchel's a great showman, but he's not a team man."

He strikes a match and puffs on a cigar.

"What about Bell? He wouldn't have to hit, just play centerfield and steal everything but your jock straps. Plus these guys would play real cheap."
COMISKEY

"Son, I held Jesse James' horse when I was a boy in Missoura. I started playing ball in eighteen eighty-one. I've seen millions of players come and go. (He blows a smoke ring.) But I've never seen one black boy who was good enough to play major league baseball. They just don't see the same kind of pitching we've got up here.

"And another thing: They don't have the moral values it takes to play in the big leagues."
Burns scribbles notes.
COMISKEY

"This is off the record."
BURNS

(Putting his pencil down) "But, Charlie, this isn't eighteen-eighty-one, This is nineteen-thirty-nine. Times are different now."

"Are they? Have you ever seen any colored cops on the street? When you go shopping at Marshall Field, do you see any Negro sales girls? Any black folks live in your neighborhood?"
Burns shakes his head.

"Why do they want baseball to do something that nobody else will do?"

"Somebody's gotta be the first."
COMISKEY

"If I see one black boy who shows me he's got the right stuff, I'll be the first to sign him. But in my opinion, you and I will never see the day any of them will play in the major leagues."

Comiskey and Flanagan go into Comiskey's inner office.

FLANAGAN

"I thought you liked Samson and Paige. We could sure use 'em."

COMISKEY

"There's too many of 'em. One or two might be okay. But we can't open the doors to them all. What would my southern players say if I fired one of their buddies and gave his job to a black boy? And how can we put him in the same hotel with the rest of the club?"

FLANAGAN

"They've got a lot of fans. Did you see how many there were at the game? Fifty thousand. We haven't had a crowd that big since the World Series in nineteen-nineteen."

"Yeah, but they'd drive the white fans away. And you'd have a race riot on your hands if a black boy slides too hard into a white guy. No, the white customers will never accept blacks sitting next to them. Besides, they're good tenants. They make money for me when my club is on the road."

He gives Flanagan a wink.

Part V

1942

MULE'S APARTMENT

The radio plays "I Don't Want to Walk Without You, Baby." Mule and Clara sit at the kitchen table, baby Effie in a high chair spoons oatmeal onto her chin. Clara wipes it off. A letter sits on the table between them.

CLARA

"You've got to go, dear. "

MULE

"It don't make sense. I can play ball in Cuba; I can't play in the big leagues in America. But I gotta fight for America. It don't make sense."

She reaches for his hand. "Don't worry about us. I can stay with Aunt Matilda in Akron. They're hiring women in the rubber plants for war work."

They sit wordlessly.

A RAILWAY CAR

The sound track plays "Chattanoga Choo-Choo." Mule, Clara, and Effie sit by a window as the train glides to a stop in front of a sign saying, "Louisville." Three soldiers - a sergeant , a corporal, and a PFC - with duffel bags over their shoulders enter the car.

CORPORAL

"Heh, boy, you're in seats."

Mule looks around at several empty seats and digs into his pocket for their tickets.

"Those tickets ain't no good. You're in Tennessee now, boy. You're in the wrong car; this is for white folks. (He dumps his duffle on the seat opposite.)

"That's your car, up there." (He jerks his thumb toward the engine, which is belching smoke.) "Move it, boy, you know what you're supposed to do.

Mule starts to rise. "Yeah, I know what I'm supposed to do." He suddenly uncoils a punch. The sergeant sprawls onto the next seat. The private doubles his fist and rushes Mule. Other passengers cry out. Two civilians dash forward, as does the conductor.

CORPORAL

"Okay, hold it.... Hold it!" (He shoves the PFC aside and tells the other passengers:) "Okay, folks. Everything's all right."

With exaggerated slowness, Mule helps Clara gather her bag, pulls their other luggage from the overhead rack, and follows her up the aisle.

They pass a line of men in fatigue uniforms boarding the car, speaking German. Mule turns to see a big "POW" stenciled on each man's back.

In the Jim Crow car, Clara and Effie sit alone. Two rows ahead, Mule is also sitting by himself. She gets up and walks toward him.

CLARA

"Honey? You okay? Don't you want to sit with us?"

He turns his head away toward the window. The reflection shows tears of rage on his cheek. She touches his shoulder lightly and walks back to the baby. Mule stares at the landscape rushing by.

FRANCE

A snowy day. A line of Army trucks slips and slides along a muddy road as artillery shells burst in the nrby hills. Each explosion of light is followed a few seconds later by a roar. One truck's wheel slides into a rut, the tires spinning. The driver curses and double clutches, rocking back and forth. Finally, it climbs out, spitting mud and ice behind.

It pulls into a truck park, and the driver, wearing corporals' stripes, swings down from the cab, beating his arms to keep warm, his breath coming in clouds.

It is Mule.

He joins a line of drivers trudging toward a corrugated tin quonset hut. Inside he picks up a metal tray next to a pile of Stars And Stripes newspapers with the headline
GERMAN BLITZ TAKES
HEAVY TOLL In BULGE

The men shuffle along a chow line as explosions continue to rumble outside. The meal finished, Mule and his buddy, Hank, lean back and drain the last of their cans of beer. Mule burps just as a shell outside explodes like thunder.

Man!" says Hank. "That was some fart!"

A black sergeant walks in and shouts "Ten-HUT!" Everyone jumps to his feet as a white colonel enters, saying, "Be seated." He colonel reads from a clipboard.

"Army is taking a beating in Belgium - they call it 'the Bulge.' I've just received the following message from Supreme Allied Headquarters in Paris." He reads:

Supreme Headquarters
Allied Expeditionary Force
The United States Army is happy to offer to a limited number of Negro privates the privilege of joining our veteran units at the front to give you the opportunity of fighting shoulder to shoulder to bring about victory.

NCOs may accept reduction in rank in order to take advantage of this opportunity.

(signed)
Dwight D Eisenhower
General
commanding

"Any questions?"

Hank looks around. He raises his hand. "Uh, sir, they mean, 'infantry,' right?"

"That's what it sounds like."

Another hand goes up. "How come we have to get busted to private?"

COLONEL

"I don't know any more than you do."

The men murmur. Hank leans over and whispers: "They don't want no black guys giving orders to no white guys."

The sergeant calls attention, and the colonel leaves.

SERGEANT

"I'll put this sign-up sheet on the bulletin board. All those interested can put your names on it."

The men break into groups, talking.

HANK

"Man, I want to get me some *krauts*!"

Mule wrestles with the choice. At length he shrugs, "OK," and they join the line at the bulletin board.

GERMANY

Mule, wearing the patch of the 45th "Thunderbird" Division of the Oklahoma National Guard, squints through binoculars. He turns to a radio man.

MULE

"Add one hundred meters, left fifty. Ten rounds, high explosive. Fire for effect."

Across the valley the rounds explode on an enemy gun position. The gun flies into the air, along with a motorcycle and parts of bodies.

Mule pokes his head out of his foxhole to look. A line of machine gun rounds - <u>brrrrt</u> - stitches a trail on the ground. He pulls his head back just in time.

"Almost got beaned that time."

A TOWN IN GERMANY

Mule saunters among bombed out buildings, idly girl-watching, when he is tackled from the rear. He wrestles free and whirls around to find a white GI grinning and hugging him.

MULE
"Bobby! You redneck cracker!"

BOBBY
"Mule! You ol' muscle-bound coal miner!"

They wrestle some more.

MULE
"What's the matter? You don't write to your old buddies? Don't the Cardinals have mail boxes?"

"How the hell can anyone find you? You're all over the map."

"Got to go where the money is, Buddy. They don't dish it out to us like they do to you."

"How's ol' Jud?"

"Still mean as a horny bear."

"Cool?"

"Still fast as a coon in heat."

"And Ramon?

"Handsome as a dog with pups."

"Duty?"

"Oh, he's still chasin' 'em as much as ever, but I think they're runnin' faster than they used to."

They turn into a *bistro*. It's noisy and smoky and filled with GI's. The juke box plays "They Call it the Jersey Bounce (the rhythm That really counts)." Bobby and Mule push their way in. GI's at the bar swivel around and growl.

"Who the hell let you in?... Go to your own damn bar... Where the hell you think you are?"

MULE

"Heh, this is Germany, man, not America."

Bobby steps between them and steers Mule to a booth. A waitress sets down two beers. They clink bottles and drink. Bobby spies a Stars and Stripes newspaper and idly turns to the back page.

BOBBY

"Heh, Mule! Look!"

The headline reads:

DODGERS SIGN FIRST NEGRO

Mule grabs it and reads.

BOBBY

"Didn't I tell ya? Didn't I say you were gonna get in some day?"

MULE

"Yeah, that's right, you did, Bob."

Both read intently.

MULE

"Robinson?... Robinson? Who the hell is Jackie Robinson? I never heard of no Jackie Robinson."

"It says he's a football player."

"How come they pick some football player? I'm the king. Why didn't they pick me?"

"It says he played with white boys, Mule."

"I played with white boys - Dizzy Dean, Jimmie Foxx. Who did Robinson ever play with?"

"It says he went to college."

"What do you mean, college? I went to Wilkinson's College. I've seen the world. I been to Mexico, I been to Dominica, I been to Cuba. That boy Robinson ever been there? What's he know out of books I don't know out of life? I could write the books he reads in his old college.

"Where was he while I was fightin'?"

Bob consults the paper. "It says he was playin' ball with the Monarchs."

"Playin' <u>ball</u>?!"

"Yeah, he got discharged before his outfit went overseas."

"He *did*!? How come?"

Bobby shrugs. "It doesn't say. But he's twenty-five, Mule."

"Yeah. And I'm thirty-three. And Satch is about forty."

"You're the king of Negro baseball, Mule. And Satch is still the king of the pitchers. Everybody knows that."

"You mean "were," Bob. We <u>were</u> the kings."
                    BOBBY

"I'm   "I'm still the fastest pitcher in the big leagues, and I'm going back next year and prove it. And you're still the hardest hitter in baseball. Robinson can't hit 'em as far two-handed as you can one-handed. And I want you to go back and prove it too."

"Yeah?"

"Yeah!"

"You mean maybe I can play for the Cardinals?"

"They don't have anybody any better, Mule. Hell, they don't have anybody half as <u>good</u>!"

"Yeah, that's for damn sure!"

Mule downs the rest of his bottle in one long gulp, wipes his mouth with his wrist, and lets out a yelp. All talk in the bar stops, and all heads swing toward him.

"Yeeeow! Who's the greatest damn hitter ever?"

Bobby raises his bottle: "Babe Ruth!"

Mule shoots him a black look.

"You and Babe Ruth."

Mule puts a friendly hammerlock on Bobby.

"Who?"

"You and Josh Gibson."

Mule tightens the lock."<u>Who</u>?"
                    BOBBY
(Gasping:)"You!"
"Who am I?"
(Laughing and choking:) "Mule!"
"Mule <u>who</u>?"
"Mule Samson!"
 Everybody has turned to look.

                    MULE
"Tell 'em who hit the longest ball in
baseball history, almost clear out of
Yankee Stadium! <u>Tell</u> 'em!"
"You did, Mule!"

                    MULE
(Letting him up): "Who's the home run champeen of
the world?"

                    BOBBY
(Lifting his bottle). "To Mule Samson - the home
run champeen of the world!" (They clink bottles.)
"Kick, Mule!"
Mule gives the wall a smash with his foot. He
mugs and struts and flexes his arms. When he has
everyone's attention, he gives the wall a thumping
punch and leaves a hole clear through it.

A RURAL BALL FIELD

The sound track plays "Spring Is Bustin' Out All
Over." It is the same ball field in the Kansas town
we saw near the beginning of the film. Players are
hitting fungoes, playing "pepper," etc. Mule appears
heavier, out of shape.
                    COOL
"Heh, big man! How 'bout that Jackie? Hitting
good up there in Montreal. We're old-timers now, huh,
Mule? Everybody's forgotten us."
                    MULE
"Forgot, hell! They never <u>knew</u> about us. We were
born twenty years too soon. 'Welcome back, buddy.

While you were fightin' Hitler, somebody stole your life."

Cool and Candy (who is now graying) exchange looks and move away.

COOL

"He's been like this since he's been back."

"What do you think he's on? Reefers?"

"I think it's worse than that, Skip."

Mule drives a batting practice pitch over the trees, steps out of the batting cage.

A new kid, Willie, steps in. He is 18 and lithe as a running back. He hits one almost to the tree.

COOL

"Heh, Mule, that your old tree. Better tell him not to mess with the your tree.

"Who's he?

"Some kid out of high school, named Willie somethin' or other."

In centerfield Cool and Willie stand together. A ball is hit deep, and Cool flies back, his hat blowing off, turns, and makes a basket catch at his waist. Another fly, a little deeper, and Willie lopes back effortlessly, making a graceful over-the-shoulder catch.

CLUBHOUSE

The radio plays "It's been a long, long time." Mule and Cool slump wearily on their benches, slowly removing tape from their leagues until they look like two mummies with rolls of tape at their feet.

Willie, almost naked in the center of the room, cavorts, snapping his towel at the other players.

MULE

"Who the hell's he think he is?"

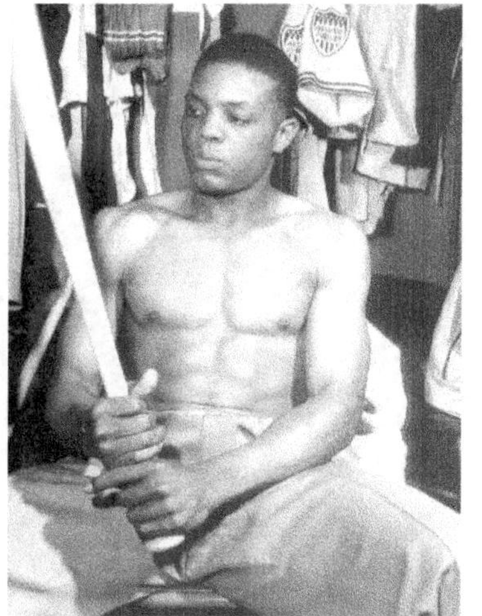

COOL

"He'll be great some day. But he doesn't know anything about playin' the hitters. And he doesn't even look where the fence is."

"Yeah. And he's afraid of the curve."

MINOR LEAGUE PARK

Sound cue: "You Won't Be Satisfied Until You Break My Heart." Comiskey and Flanagan stand at the batting cage, watching Mule smash some long ones. As he leaves the cage, Comiskey calls to him. He and Cool jog over.

COMISKEY

"Hello, boys. Glad to see you again." (They nod.) "I'm down here looking for players. You got a lot of good ones.

Eddie Montague joins them. "Hi. I'm Eddie Montague, scout for the Giants. You the man they call 'the black Babe Ruth?'"

COOL

"You mean Ruth was 'the white Mule Samson.'"

MONTAGUE

"How old are ya now, Mule?"

MULE

"Thir- "

COOL

- "Twenty-seven."

MONTAGUE

"Too bad I didn't see you a few years sooner."

MULE

(Spitting): "I been here all the time."

A shout goes up, and they turn to the outfield to look. Willie makes a great catch, banging into the fence. He picks himself off the ground and trots back to the dugout. Comiskey, Flanagan, and Montague hurry over to him.

COMISKEY

"Too bad. Those two were real good before the war. But (he clicks his tongue) I can't take a chance on them now. I need fellows with a future."

Mule and Cool, still in ear-shot, turn slowly away.

MULE

"Now it's okay to be black if you're young, and it's okay to be old if you're white. But it ain't okay to be black <u>and</u> old. Now, I can beat bein' black. But how'm I gonna beat bein' old?"

Wilkinson has come out on the field and steps between Comiskey and Willie.

"Just a minute, Charlie. These are my ball players. You want to talk to them, talk to me first."

"Oh? You got a contract with these boys?"

"I've always treated my players up-and-up. Ask them, they'll tell you."

"Wilkie, I like you. But your league is run by racketeers like Greenlee. What have you ever done for baseball?"

WILKIE

(Starting to fume:) "Who was the first team to play night baseball when you said it would never work? <u>We</u> were. Who showed you how to save your hides when you didn't have a dime to pay the mortgage? <u>I</u> did."

The usually mid-mannered Wilkinson is warming up. Much shorter than Comiskey, he lifts his face and sputters.

"Where were you when these boys needed a job? I didn't see you giving 'em one. Where were you when I needed help meeting a payroll? I didn't I see you giving me any. If I hadn't mortgaged my home and put my life savings on the line all those years, there wouldn't be any of these players for you to come sniffing around trying to steal."

COMISKEY

"Take it easy, Wilkie. This is America. I can talk to them if I want to."

"These are _my_ players, Charlie. You try to monkey around with them, I'll haul you into court!"

"The Negro press will have your head if you try it, and you know it."

Wilkinson is so mad he can only sputter.

Comiskey laughs.

The players, who are taking all this in, break into groups, whispering.

At the batting cage, Willie ducks away from a curve ball.

                         COOL

"Why don't you show him how to stand up to a curve, roomie?"

                         MULE

(Spits.) "Hell, he's so damn good, let him teach himself."

Practice over, the players file off the field. Cool falls in step next to Willie.

                         COOL

"Kid, you're 'trailin' the ball. You're gonna break your head open bangin' into fences. Let me show you how to do it."

They return to the outfield. Candy Jim hits a fungo to them. Cool turns his back on home plate, runs to the fence, turns and waits for the ball to settle into his glove in a basket catch. Willie tries it. He misjudges the first two balls, one of which falls short, the other falls to his left.

                         COOL

"Don't worry, kid. You'll get the hang of it. Listen to the bat; it'll tell you where the ball's gonna go. Then run there and turn around. If it's over the fence, you won't be able to catch it anyway."

Willie tries a couple more and catches both of them easily.

WILLIE

"How'd you catch it like this?" He imitates the basket catch.

"Just practice."

Another ball is hit. Cool moves under it, bends forward, and makes a basket catch behind his back. Willie's eyes pop.

COOL

"One more thing."

He takes off Willie's cap and puts his own on the boy's head. It's a size too small.

"Now try it again."

Another fungo goes up, and Willie races back, his hat flying off.

"That's it, kid! Those newspaper guys love that stuff."

Later Cool and Mule watch Willie at bat, falling away from a curve. Benny is on the mound. Candy lays a bat down behind Willie, who pulls away from the curve and stumbles on the bat. Candy patiently puts the bat back and nods to Benny to throw again.

Benny pitches, Willie stumbles... Benny pitches, Willie swings... Benny pitches, Willie hits a line drive to center. Cool smiles. Mule grimaces sourly.

A MAJOR LEAGUE PARK

Willie cracks a homer. In the dugout, Cool leans over to Mule.

"He's catching you. Only two homers behind now."

"Ah, the kid got lucky."

A BAR

The players are having some beers, bantering with girls. Duke Ellington's "It Don't Mean a Thing If It Ain't Got That Swing" plays in the background. Mule drops a shot of whiskey into his beer glass and knocks the drink back.

A customer jabs him with a finger.

"Heh, what about that Jackie Robinson? Got two more hits for Montreal."

MULE

"Hell, who he ever hit against? Smoky Joe? Bullet Joe? Big Bill Foster?"

"Smoky who? Bullet who?"

"Williams! Rogan! Ain't you ever heard of Satchel Paige?

"That ol' clown? He's washed up, man. I'm talkin' real baseball, none of that clown stuff."

"Washed up? He could drive nails with his fastball! Ain't that true, boys?

PLAYERS

"Yeah, man ... Damn right. You tell 'im!"

COOL

"You ever hear of Mule Samson?"

"Yeah, my daddy told me 'bout him. He was pretty good when he was alive."

MULE

"Alive?! Stand up!"

The man slides off his stool, grinning. Mule stoops, grabs the man's ankles and, with a grunt, lifts him up and stands him on the bar. The man's eyes pop.

"Call that dead? Can Jackie Robinson do that?"

Mule pushes his way through the patrons and lurches into the men's room. Cool runs after him, but the door slams in his face. He knocks.

"Heh, Mule. Come on out. Mule?"

He returns to the bar, shaking his head.

"It's those damn reefers, man."

The men's room door opens, and the players rush over to mule. He is slobbering and shakes them off. He stumbles, and the players pick him up under his armpits. He swings wildly and pushes them away, shouting and slurring his words. They wrestle him out of the bar.

HOTEL ROOM

Cool and the others sit on the edges of their beds. "Full Moon And Empty Arms" in the background. From outside the room they hear Mule's voice.

"Heh, Joe! Why won't ya talk to me, huh?..."

They rush into his room. He is sitting on the open window ledge, his feet dangling out.

"What's-a matter, huh, Joe? Talk to me! Think you're too good, huh?... Heh, DiMaggio, say something."

The players pull him back inside.

HOSPITAL CORRIDOR

The sound track plays "Don't Fence Me In." Clara, Wilkinson, Candy Jim, and a doctor stand outside Mule's room.

WILKIE

(To Clara:) "You better let us go in first. I know he doesn't want you to see him like this."

They open the door and enter.

PADDED CELL

Mule is sitting on the bed, his arms wrapped in a strait jacket. He is subdued and glowering. Wilkie puts a hand on his shoulder. Mule tugs at his jacket.

CANDY

"Pretty rough time, huh, buddy?"

Mule tugs mightily.

WILKIE

"The doc says the medicine's doing you good. You've got to get that stuff out of your body."

Mule tugs.

DOCTOR

"You're coming along, Mule. The first few days are hell. You want to play ball?"

Mule nods and strains. "Yeah."

                    CANDY

"We need you, man. Satch and the Crawfords will be here Saturday."

                    DOCTOR

"If you'll stay on the medication, you can go home tomorrow. Is it a deal?"

Mule nods.

                    CANDY

"All the boys are waitin' for ya, Mule. They want to see you kick again like the old days."

                    DOCTOR

"Your wife's outside. I'll just take this thing off, and you can go out and see her."

Before the doctor can move, Mule gives a shout and a mighty tug. One shoulder seam rips loose. He pulls one arm free, rips the other sleeve off at the shoulder, and stands with his fists in the air.

He bursts out of the room, seizes Clara, and gives her a passionate kisses.

                  BALL PARK

In batting practice Mule swings. The ball rips between the pitcher's legs. He swings again. The ball spins the shortstop around. He swings again. The ball sails between the outfielders.

The players whoop and clap their hands.

                   PLAYERS

"Kick, Mule!... The big man's back!... Wouldn't you like to see him when he's feelin' _good_? ... Man, give me some of that medicine too!"

                    COOL

(To Willie:) "Look at the old man. You shoulda seen him when he was your age, kid. Keep on hittin' like you are, boy, and you can kick like the Mule yourself some day."

The Pittsburgh _Courier_ banner headline says:

           MONTREAL FANS HAIL JACKIE

In smaller type at the bottom of the page:

Samson Socks
Two Home Runs

The <u>Afro-American</u> banner reads:
ROBINSON STEALS TWO BASES
The one-column head in the lower left says:
Mule Blasts
500-Footer
In Stadium

The Chicago <u>Defender</u>:
JACKIE LEADING MONTREAL TO FLAG
Mule Trails Mayberry
By One In Homer Race

YANKEE STADIUM

Yankee Stadium by Andy Jurinko ©2008 Bill Goff Inc.

The sound track plays Sinatra singing "New York, New York (If you can make it there, you'll make it anywhere ...)" A sparse crowd lolls in the seats. Candy and Wilkinson talk on the sidelines.
CANDY
"Man, where's all the people at?"
"They're all over in Jersey City to see Jackie play with Montreal. We can't even draw <u>flies</u>."

The players clatter up the runway from the locker room and onto the field. Cool and Mule are side by side.

                              COOL
"The kid's pushing you, huh, roomie?"
                              MULE
"Yeah. But I can take him. I want to win the title one more time."
                              COOL
"The kid has a shot in the majors. Hell, you've got plenty of titles, one more won't matter. This could be Willie's ticket."

"Nobody gave _me_ a ticket."

"Why don't ya let him look good? The scouts are all here to see him."

"Well, maybe they want to see _me_."

"It means big money for him."

"Nobody gave _me_ big money. I'm better than these young sombitches ever _will_ be. If I can win one more, they'll have to sign me."

There is a sudden cry.

"Nancy!"

Buck turns, and Satchel trots over. They slap hands.

                              BUCK
"Satchel! You still pitchin'? What is this, a ball team or a home for old ladies?"

                             SATCHEL
"You can throw away that bat, you ain't gonna hit nothin' today."
                              COOL
"We're gonna bunt you right out of the game. Lay one down here, lay one over there, see how good you can bend over. You'll be puffin' and cryin' before the first inning's over."

"No you ain't either, Little Speedy, 'cause you ain't even gonna see my 'Trouble Ball.'"

MULE

"Hell, old man, that ain't nothin' but a nickel curve. I hit four hundred against that dinky little thing ten years ago."

"Yeah, but you ain't gonna <u>see</u> it, 'cause you ain't even gonna be <u>lookin'</u> at it."

"What you mean, man?"

"'Cause I got me a secret weapon."

COOL

"Stop jiving us, man. What 'secret weapon'"?

"It ain't a pitch, it's my new owner."

He nods toward a front-row box seat. To the tune of "You Must Have Been a Beautiful Baby ('cause, Baby, look at you now),"

Mrs Manley, stunning in a low-cut jacket, is smiling broadly and showing her profile to the fans, who stand in line for autographs while others behind them whistle and make various animal noises. She tosses her head and waves. Then she crosses her legs and bends forward to straighten her stocking. More whistles and cheering from her fans.

SATCH

"You better not even sneak a peek, or I'll shoot my 'Alabama Aspirin' by you."

Willie trots out of the dugout past them.

"Wait'll these young kids see my 'Be Ball' – it be where I <u>want</u> it to be. Willie here thinks he's goin' to the big leagues, but he just might have to wait a year or two."

Comiskey and Montague come over and shake hands.

MONTAGUE

"You ever play here before, Mule?"

                              COOL
    "You kiddin'? They ought to call this 'The House
that <u>Mule</u> Built.' (He points.) See that exit ramp on
the third deck? The last one on the right? Mule
kicked one into that ramp off Lefty Gomez. Took
forty-five minutes to climb up there after the game.
Gomez bought some glasses. Next time he saw Mule, he
threw them away, it scared him so much.
    (He points to the bleachers.) "Mule, where did
your home run almost go out?"
    "See that bullpen, between the bleachers and the
stands? Almost over the back wall."
    The camera zooms in.

                              COOL
    "They measured it - five hundred fifteen feet."
                              MONTAGUE

                    "How old were you then, Mule?"
                    (Modestly:) "Eighteen."
                    "Wow! Too bad I didn't see you
              then!"
                    "Well, I been here all the
              time."
                    Clara and Effie, now five in a
              new pink dress, take their seats.
              Clara holds Effie up to wave to
              Daddy.
                    Montague takes a seat in the
president's box, loosens his tie, and takes out his
pad and pencil.

                           ANNOUNCER
    "We've got a special treat for you today - the
owner the New York Black Yankees... the man loved we
world-wide for dancing with Shirley Temple in the
movies...the world's top tap dancer - Bill
"Bojangles" Robinson!
    The dancer and his diminutive partner spring to
the top of the dugout, the PA strikes up, "On the

good ship, Lollipop," and the two go into the famous movie routine to great applause.

As they boogey off, Duty, wearing a white doctor's jacket, strides to the mound and sets up a folding chair. From his pocket he produces a carpenter's drill and an over-size pair of garden pliers.

Skinny, his jaw wrapped in bandages, staggers out of the dugout, holding his head in agony. Duty sits him down and opens his mouth wide. Skinny lets out a muffled yelp and tries to escape, but Duty pushes him back down. He brings out the drill, Skinny shakes his head in terror. Duty puts a knee on Skinny's thigh and wields the pliers while Skinny kicks wildly.

Meanwhile, Benny tiptoes up behind with a giant firecracker, puts it under the chair, then puts his fingers in his ears. BANG! Skinny leaps up and races away, spitting a mouthful of corn as he goes.

The crowd thinks it's side-splitting. Effie claps and laughs.

ANNOUNCER

"Last game of the season, folks. The Monarchs have already clinched the title behind their sensational rookie, Willie Mayberry, and a terrific comeback by their great veteran, Mule Samson. The big question is, which one will win the home run race? Mayberry is ahead by one."

The soundtrack plays "September Song (The days dwindle down to a precious few)." Mule kneels on deck. Willie stands in the box, waggling his bat. Satchel goes into a windmill windup, twists his body, and brings his lead foot down. Willie begins his swing. Satch then whips his arm around and releases the ball, but Willie is already out in front. He hits a weak tap to first base. The crowd groans.

Montague shakes his head and smiles. "I'll be a son of a gun. The old 'Hesitation Pitch.'"

As Mule steps into the box, he hears a familiar whistle. It's Jud, taking a seat behind home. He flashes Mule a thumbs up.

Satch pitches, and Mule hits a grounder through the box; the second baseman goes far to his right, backhands it, and throws him out.

Clara slumps in her seat.

Mule trots to the dugout, kicks the water cooler, and sits down hard next to Cool.

ANNOUNCER

"Mayberry is still ahead. If he can hold that lead, he's a sure bet to win a contract to the big leagues."

Fourth inning. Willie walks up to bat. Satchel grins, raises his foot high, and fires. Willie swings and drives a screamer to deep center.

The fans leap to their feet.

The center fielder races back and takes the ball over his shoulder at the 481-foot sign. The crowd groans.

Montague drops his pad to his lap and leans back in his seat.

Mule is up. He pounds the plate.

Clara bites her lip.

Mule pounds the plate.

Satch grins, then delivers.

Mule gives a mighty grunt and swings. The crack echoes through the vast park. Pitcher and batter both watch the ball streak on a low line toward the leftfield bleachers at the 405-foot mark.

Clara leaps up with the rest of the crowd, holding

Effie up to see, cheering and crying at the same time.

The fielder follows the ball to the gate and watches it sail over his head and deep into the bleachers.

ANNOUNCER

"That was over five hundred feet, folks. Even Babe Ruth never hit one there!"

Mule goes into a home run trot. Satchel watches him round third and lifts his hat in salute. Mule salutes back. At home, he jumps heavily on the plate. Josh extends a hand. The two embrace.

Mule disappears into the dugout, but the crowd calls him back, and he waves his hat.

The players clap him on the back and rub his head. Mule sits down hard next to Cool. He speaks to Cool but loud enough for Willie to hear.

"Man, Satch is <u>bringin'</u> it! You can't pull that outside fastball, you just waste your power hittin' it to center."

Ninth inning.

ANNOUNCER

"Well, this is it. Last of the ninth. Mayberry and Samson are all tied up."

Willie knocks the dirt out of his cleats with his bat, steps in, and taps the plate. Josh pounds his glove, Satchel smiles cunningly and throws one on the outside corner. Willie pulls his bat back and takes strike one.

JOSH

"What's the matter, kid? Too fast for you?" (To Paige:) "He can't even see it, Satch."

Josh sets an outside target, then moves at the last second to the inside corner. Willie swings. The ball arches up into the sky and falls in the leftfield grandstand.

Montague and the rest of the crowd stand and holler.

Mule is swinging his bat in the on-deck circle. He leans down to pick up a resin bag as Willie passes him. The others mob Willie with slaps, embraces, and pats on the rump.

ANNOUNCER

"You did it, kid!... All <u>right</u>!..."

Willie gives the fans a wave of his hat, sits down and towels his head.

SKINNY

"Wait'll they see you ON THE Giants, kid!"

BUCK

"You're the best, boy! You're the king, you're the new champ!"

COOL

"Not yet, he ain't."

All turn to watch Mule.

FAN

"Give her one more kick, Mule!"

Clara squeezes Effie's hand.

Mule squeezes the bat handle. His jaw tenses. He stares hard at Satchel. Slowly, purposefully, Paige pumps, and raises his foot. In slow motion, Satchel's arm comes around, and the pitch comes toward Mule. Mule's shoulders dip as he begins his swing. There is a loud KEE-RACK as the ball begins to climb, up, up, up.

Then down, down, down, nestling into the shortstop's glove.

The players leap up and embrace Willie.

PLAYERS

"Way to go, kid!.... Heh, champ!... My man! etc."

Almost unnoticed, Mule enters the dugout. Willie turns toward him and hesitates awkwardly. He starts to extend his hand and speak.

                    MULE
(Cutting him off:) "Nice goin', kid."
     He brushes past without stopping, picks up his glove, and walks into the runway.
     Cool catches up and searches his friend's face, but it's a blank.
                    COOL
     "That was a real nice - "
                    MULE
     "Go to hell."
     The rest of the team follows, still clapping Willie on the back. Montague and Comiskey sprint after Willie. Montgue gets there first and bumps Comiskey, who stumbles and falls.
                  MONTAGUE
     "Willie! Got a minute?"
     Willie stops. The rest of the players walk on ahead, looking back over their shoulders as Comiskey wheezes up, bumps into a player, and stumbles again. They watch Willie and Al huddle, framed in the doorway of the tunnel.
     Willie catches up with his teammates.
                   WILLIE
     "Man, let's get a shower and <u>celebrate</u>!"
                   CANDY
     (Laughing:) "Hell, you ain't in the big leagues yet, Kid. When you get in the big time, then you're <u>Mister</u> Mayberry, and you can wash where the big leaguers wash. Now you're still Willie the Kid, and you wash with the colored folks, back at the Y."
     Their bus rolls up in front of a Harlem YMCA. Several bulbs on the sign are missing. The players spill out and troop inside.
     They jostle outside the shower. Then they back away and let Mule go in first.
                    MULE
     "Where's the Kid? The Kid goes first!"
     He pulls Willie forward and pushes him in.

A NIGHTCLUB

As the band plays "Take the A-Train," the team members are celebrating. Willie is the center of attention, with several women surrounding him.

Mule and Clara sit together at a booth, two shot glasses in front of Mule. He takes one and knocks it back. Clara takes his hand.

CLARA

"Please, honey."

Mule ignores her, knocks the second one back, and calls to the bartender.

"Two more!"

Willie breaks away and walks over to their table.

(Hesitantly:) "Mind if I sit down?"

Mule says nothing, but Clara smiles, and Willie slides across from Mule.

WILLIE

"You should have been the first, Mule. I'll never be able to carry your bat, I know that. You were born twenty years too soon."

Mule thinks it over.

"Nah. I was born right on time. Suppose I was born twenty years later. I would have had different parents. I wouldn't be George Samson. I might have been a skinny kid with some disease, couldn't play ball. I would never have married my wife. I wouldn't have had my kid. Would I want to change all that?"

WILLIE

"I'm scared, Mule. I wish you were coming with me."

Mule doesn't answer.

"Will they let me in the same hotel with the other guys? What if the pitchers throw at me? What if the umpires don't give me the close strikes? What if I get in a slump? Will they send me down?"

Mule continues to listen without comment.

"The fans will boo. What will the newspapers say? What about the other guys on the team? If I take their friend's job, they aren't gonna like that... What if I fail? What'll that do to the guys comin' up after me? I'm worried, Mule."

Mule eyes him for several seconds.

"Just remember one thing, Kid." (Pause):

"Where you're going ain't half as tough as where you been."

                    HOTEL LOBBY

"Missouri Waltz" plays in the background as Wilkinson sits in an armchair. Candy, Skinny, and Buck are standing. They all look somber as Cool and Mule stroll in.

                       COOL

"What's up?...Something wrong?"

                      WILKIE

"I'm afraid this is the end of the road, boys. I just can't do it any more."

                       COOL

"What do you mean?"

"The league is dead. I'm out of money." (Murmurs from the players.) "Mayberry is gone. They're taking Connie Johnson, my new pitcher ... And my shortstop, the kid from Texas that Buck found – Ernie Banks."

                      SKINNY

"Yeah, but you got some good dough for them ...."

Wilkinson pulls his pockets inside out. "This is it. And a basket of fruit." (He nods to a table with the basket on it.) "It's like coming into a man's store and stealing all the goods right off the shelves."

The players shift weight but can't think of anything to say.

                      WILKIE

"They say we're gangsters and racketeers, so it's okay to take our players without paying for them.

Rickey never put out a penny for Jackie or Willie or anyone else he wanted."

                    CANDY

    "They're the real racketeers."

                    BUCK

    "You never treated anybody like that, Mister Wilkinson."

                    JUD

    "You can't just let them rob you like that."

                    WILKIE

    "If I object, they'd drop Willie like a hot foul ball. They never paid a nickel for all the Negro players they've taken - Robinson, Camanella, Newcombe. They know they can get away with it - the commissioner won't do anything about it."

                    CANDY

    "You can sue."

                    WILKIE

    (Shaking his head, then slowly): "No. I won't stand in a man's way if he has a chance to better himself."

    They stare at the floor, wrapped in memories. The sound track softly plays "These foolish things (remind me of you)."

                    WILKIE

    "How many years have we been traveling the prairies together? Fifteen? Twenty? Thirty? I remember back in nineteen nineteen, the All Nations team. We had a Hawaiian, an Indian, two Cubans, even a girl. We'd sleep in tents and go fishing for dinner.

    "If it rained a lot, I had to mortgage my house to make the pay roll."

    Candy and Buck nod silently.

                    WILKIE

    "Candy, you remember the night after we played Grover Alexander's House of David team and we had a

tire blowout? We had to drive all the way back to Pine Bluff to buy another tire."
CANDY
(Laughing): "I was holding it on the running board and I fell asleep and let it roll away."
WILKIE
(Chuckles): "We had to make a forty-mile round-trip back to get another one. Boy, were we mad at you!"
Candy wipes his eyes from laughter.
CANDY
"That ol' bus. Didn't even have an emergency exit in back. Everybody had a box under the seat with salami and bread for lunch.. . Yeah, those were the good old days, huh, J.L.?
"Yep. I still remember the day Skinny came up to me in Neshoba Kansas and asked for a job."
SKINNY
"I didn't even have shoes on."
"I had to buy you a pair."
"Yeah. I nailed spikes to the heels of my street shoes and had to walk all tilted forward. Had to learn to walk all over again."
Candy and Skinny are both laughing.
CANDY
"And how many times did we get rained out for a week, and we couldn't pay the landlady?"
BUCK
"Yeah, she called the sheriff, and he sold our car at auction right on the street in front of her house."
WILKIE
(Grinning): "Yep. She got twenty-five dollars for it. We had to cancel the rest of the season."
More laughter.
WILKIE
"But I never missed a payday. Had to mortgage my house, but you fellows got paid on time."

EVERYONE

(Nodding): "That's true.... Sure did."

COOL

"And you lent money to the other teams to meet their payrolls and keep the league going."

CANDY

(Still laughing:) "I don't know, J.L. You probably owe me a million dollars by now."

WILKIE

(Blowing his nose hard): "I owe you a million dollars just for the fun we had. We've seen a lot of history come and go, haven't we? Those days will never come again."

Each man turns silent with his own thoughts for a moment.

SKINNY

"What's going to happen to us now, Mr Wilkinson?"

WILKIE

"I wish I knew, Skinny."

COOL

"Well, I can always go back to my winter job in politics."

BUCK

"The one at city hall?"
Cool nods.

DUTY

"You mean janitoring?"
"It's not so bad. You can live."

WILKIE

"What about you fellows?"
They look at each other.

SKINNY

"Anything we can, I guess. Don't worry about us. We'll be okay."

The sound track quietly plays "I'll Be Seeing You (in all the old familiar places)" as Wilkinson grasps each one by the hand and elbow. They silently pass in front of him, nod, and shuffle out. The screen door bangs behind each one, and he watches them trudge down the steps of the veranda.

MULE'S HOME

Doris Day is singing "It's Magic" on the radio as Mule enters, shoulders bent in discouragement. Clara is waiting in the kitchen.

"Nothin' again, Babe. Nobody's hiring. Who wants an old washed-up ballplayer?"

Clara is holding something behind her and trying to hide the big grin on her face. He folds his arms around her, clutching for the surprise. She wriggles and laughs. He finally grabs it. A telegram. He reads.

"They _want_ me! The Giants _want_ me! Me and Cool are goin' to Minneapolis!"

"Minneapolis?"

"The Giant's farm team!"

"That's where Willie is."

Mule pops a beer from the 'fridge and gurgles it down.(Beer running down his chin:) "The next stop to the major leagues! We're on our way!"

He picks Clara up and whirls her around.

PART VI.

1948

OUTSIDE MINNEAPOLIS BALLPARK

A cab pulls up. Mule and Cool pull their satchels out, then fumble for the fare. Mule carefully counts the change, then hands the cabbie a quarter. Cool snatches it away and puts a dollar in the man's hand.

Mule and Cool turn and stare at the stadium.

Lugging their bags, the two newcomers walk diffidently onto the field, where the Minneapolis Millers are warming up. The players follow them out of the corners of their eyes.

A shout. "Mule! Cool!"

Willie trots over and slaps hands.

Tommy Heath, the manager, is standing with arms folded, watching batting practice. Hearing the commotion, he walks over, hand outstretched.

HEATH

"Samson. Bell. I'm Tom Heath." He shakes their hands warmly. "We've heard a lot about you boys. Good things. I think you can help our club a lot. We're mighty glad to see you. You ready to play?"

COOL

"Man, we been ready for fifteen years."

"Good. Willie, take them down and get them fitted with uniforms. Then come back and let's see if they can hit a baseball."

He grins as Willie grabs both bags over their protests and leads them into the dugout.

They re-emerge self-consciously in new uniforms and take seats at the end of the Bench, a few spaces from the other players.

HEATH

"Mule, get up there and take a few swings."

Mule pulls his bat from its canvas case, hefts it, and steps up to the plate. The pitcher gives him a friendly nod and delivers. Mule cracks one to deep center.

He finally puts one over the scoreboard and returns to his seat near the end of the bench, but the players quickly make room for him next to them. One player, Chuck, offers his hand.

CHUCK WORKMAN

"Nice hittin', big man. Let me see that bat."

He takes a swing. "Wow! Light, isn't it?"

"Well, I just figure I can swing it faster. Try it."

Chuck walks into the batting cage, waggles the bat, and blasts a pitch against the distant fence.

CHUCK

"Heh, I think I'll get me one like this."

MULE

"You keep it, man. I got another one."

The other players crowd around with questions too.

Heath walks over. "They got a right-hander pitchin' tonight. Got a hell of a curve. How are you at hittin' curve balls?"

"Pretty good."

"Okay, I'm puttin' you in left. Think you can handle it?"

COOL
"Man, you done threw the rabbit in the briar patch."

LOUISVILLE HOTEL
The players shuffle off their bus and file through the hotel doors until only Willie, Cool, and Mule are left.

HEATH
"sorry, guys. This is Kentucky, and we got to play by the local rules. The driver will fix you up real good. We'll see you at the park tomorrow."

The bus pulls away with the three black players.

COOL
"Well, at least down South you know where you stand. Up North they say one thing but do another."

A HOME IN THE BLACK SECTION
A black man, his wife, and three kids surge out to meet them. The kids run to embrace "Uncle Willie."

Willie introduces Jesse and May.

JESSE
"Mighty proud to meet you." He shakes hands warmly. These are our young ones — Frederic and Douglas. And the little guy — I hope you don't mind — is Josh."

MULE
(In mock horror:) "Josh?! You must be a pretty good hitter. Let me feel that muscle."

Josh strikes a Tarzan pose, gritting his teeth and straining until his eyes pop.

"Man, I'm glad you're not in our league yet!" All laugh.

JESSE

"I saw you play here when I was in high school. You hit a triple. And Mister Bell caught a triple. Robbed the man like he held him up with a gun."

COOL

"If Mule hit a triple, it must have gone three miles. It takes him fifteen minutes to run to third base." More laughs.

MAY

"Well, we're very proud to have you. I hope you like fried chicken and biscuits."

COOL

"Like it? Mule led the league in eatin' chicken seven years in a row!"

She points to the fence, where the neighbors are waving and holding up children. The players go over and slap high fives and are soon signing autographs and holding babies.

INDIANAPOLIS BALLPARK

As they warm up on the sidelines, Cool suddenly calls out. "Heh, it's Schoolboy Johnny Taylor!"

He is pointing to the former Negro Leaguer. They exchange slaps.

"So, how you doin' up here, Johnny?"

"Not bad. I've pitched seven games, and they haven't beat me but once."

The game begins.

In the eighth Willie comes up. In the dugout, manager Ben Chapman shouts, "Look alive, Taylor!" and points to his head. Johnny throws a low curve for a strike.

Chapman strides to the mound. "Goddammit! Knock the nigger down."

"I know him, Skip. I can get him out."

"You do what I say, boy, or you pack your bags!" Chapman stalks back to the dugout. The catcher sets a target high and inside. Johnny throws a high fastball for strike two.

Chapman storms to the mound, waving to the bullpen. A new pitcher, Boemler, trots in. Chapman takes the ball from Tayor and slaps it into the mitt of Boemler.

Chapman: "Sit him on his ass. Got it?"

Boemler nods. He delivers one under Willie's chin. Willie pulls away and takes the pitch on his shoulder. He pretends it doesn't hurt and trots to first base.

The Minneapolis players rush onto the field, ready to fight, but the umpires and Heath finally get them back in the dugout.

Mule is next up. He drills the pitch back at Boemler's head. The pitcher falls to the ground in self-defense. Cool scores, and Willie takes second. Chuck, the next man up, lines one into the gap. Willie scores.

Mule chugs into third and makes his turn toward the plate. The throw gets away from the catcher. While the coach frantically signals "Stop!" Mule lumbers past him, head down, toward the plate. Boemler, the ball, and Mule all arrive at the same time, and Mule throws a football block into the pitcher, knocking him head over heels.

"Safe!" Boemler picks himself up and hobbles a few steps before collapsing. In the Minneapolis dugout Mule sits down heavily, cussing under his breath, as his teammates welcome him with handshakes and slaps on the back.

Cool, Willie, and Mule leave the park. They pass a man sitting on the hood of a pick-up, a shotgun resting across his knees. Above their heads two blackbirds sit together on a wire.

Taylor emerges, carrying his suitcase. They fall in step.

"How come the bag, Bill?"

"That's it, fellows. I'm goin' back to Birmingham"

"Birmingham!?"

"Yep, back to the Black Barons." He extends his hand. "Good luck. I'll be reading about you in the papers."

An awkward pause. Johnny hails a cab, picks up his bag, and gets in. Cool and Mule walk in silence for a few steps.

Suddenly a shot rings out, and a blackbird falls to the ground at their feet. Mule and Cool edge Willie onto the team bus, which pulls away.

IN A MOVIE THEATER

Mule, Cool and willie munch popcorn while a scene with the comedian Stepin Fetchit flickers on the screen. Then a message flashes on:

WILLIE MAYBERRY

REPORT TO BOX OFFICE

Willie gets up. In a moment, he returns, whispering: "I gotta go. See you later."

Next day Mule looks up and down the bench." Heh, where's Willie at?"

COOL

"Man, ain't you heard? The Giants called him up. He's on an airplane to New York."

WILLIE'S ROOM

Cool is gathering Willie's clothing and other things and dropping them into a carton. Mule enters. "Whatcha doin', man?"

"Just getting Willie's things. Gonna mail them to New York." He continues silently packing.

"When you think they're gonna call us?"

(Gently:) "They're not gonna call us, roomie." Mule looks quizzical.... "We're too old, Mule."

"Too old? Willie's hittin' three-seventy-eight. I'm hittin' three-forty. You're hittin' three-twenty-nine. I'm second in the league in homers, and you're second in stolen bases. The Giants are in a pennant race. We could win it for them."

                    COOL

"They can only take two Negroes on a team. They already got Monte Irvin. They had to let Artie Wilson go to make room for Willie. He's twenty-one. Irvin's twenty-seven. You and me are over thirty-five. They want young guys that can play another ten years."

Mule tries to make sense of it. "Then why the hell did they sign us?"

Cool feels his friend's pain. "To watch out for Willie, Mule. Keep him out of trouble."

"That's _it_?"

(Softly:) "Yeah. And some publicity."

Mule slumps onto the bed. "Damn. Couldn't they bring us up just for one day, so we could say we put our foot in a major league shoe? They said if they'd find a good player, they'd sign him."

Cool puts an arm around Mule's shoulder and says softly:

"They lied."

They both stare at the half-filled box of clothes.

MILLERS LOCKER ROOM

Mule and Cool slowly clean out their lockers. The other players come by, one by one, shake hands and mumble, "Tough luck. . ... Sorry, man."
                    CHUCK
"Good luck, guys." An awkward silence. "Uh, thanks for the loan of your bat." He hands it to Mule.
"Naw, you keep it, man. That's the only way that bat's gonna make it to the major leagues."
With a final handshake, Mule and Cool pick up their bags and walk out.

                 BAR - NIGHT
The door opens and Mule shuffles out into a winter wind, pulling his collar up, and hunches into his coat. He turns a corner and bumps into two other figures.
                     COOL
(Surprised:) "Heh, Mule, what you say?" Mule stares, confused. "It's me – me and Willie." He looks into Mule's eyes. "You okay?
Mule slowly focuses, then breaks into a grin and gives him a punch in the arm. Cool punches back. They grapple like boys.
                   WILLIE
(Softly:) "Come on, man, let's go home."
Mule shakes him away." Naw, I'm okay, man."
"No, you're not."
"I'm awright."
Willie and Cool support him and lead him into the night.

                MULE'S HOME
Clara answers the knock, and Willie and Cool enter with Mule between them. She gasps, and they lay Mule on his bed.
                   CLARA

"Honey! Where you been? I been worryin' about you."

She bends over and loosens his coat. He mumbles. She leans close to hear. Then she nods, stands, and goes into the other room, returning with his old St Louis Cardinal jacket and lays it across his chest. He nods weakly and closes his eyes.

Willie, glancing at the bare apartment, presses some bills into Clara's hand. She resists, but he gentlemen closes her fist.

HOSPITAL ROOM

Cool, Willie, Skinny, and Ramon enter with flowers and fruit. Mule is sitting up. His hair is thinner now and graying.
ALL

"Hey, my man! Lookin' good! ... Good to see ya," etc.
MULE

"Heh, guys. Thanks for coming ... Look at my kid, Willie, will ya? Fifty-one homers. That's my boy!"
WILLIE

"Hell, old man, if you played in the Polo Grounds, you'd hit seventy-five, right?"
ALL

"Yeah... You bet... No sweat."
"Nah. No more'n sixty-five."
COOL

"Sixty-<u>five</u>?! You could hit that with one hand!
"Yeah, but remember, I'm almost forty years old."

WILLIE

"Listen, Mule. You helped me out before. I need you to help me out again. I got these kids, see. It's kind of a league, you know? And I'm sort of the commissioner. Well, when you're feelin' better, can you come over and show 'em some of the things like you showed me? It'd mean a lot to them."

MULE

"The Commissioner! Well, I guess I gotta obey the commissioner, eh, boys?"

HARLEM STREET

Willie hits fungoes to kids with a broom handle and a black-taped ball. Cool is fielding the throw-ins. They stop as Mule turns a corner and walks into view.

WILLIE

"Heh, c'mere, guys. I want you to meet the greatest hitter ever lived."

The boys gather around a little shyly. Willie puts his arm around Mule. "This here's Mule Samson."

The kids look blank. "You don't know Mule Samson?"

They shake their heads. "Well, you heard of Babe Ruth, haven't you?"

They nod and giggle.

"Well, you know what we used to say? We said, 'Babe Ruth is the white Mule Samson.' That's right. You all ask your daddies. They'll tell you it's true."

The boys open their eyes wide.

"This is my teacher. Taught me everything I know about hittin'. Anything I can do, this man could do better."

The boys look at Mule with new interest.

COOL

"You been to Yankee Stadium, haven't you?"

"Yeah.... Sure."

"Well, you ever seen anybody hit a ball out of Yankee Stadium?"

They shake their heads.

"You ever hear of anybody did it?"

One boy raises his hand. "Mickey Mantle."

WILLIE

"Nah. Mickey came close. But this man hit one even farther. It took a ten-minute subway ride to reach where it hit."

There are smiles.

"I'm not kiddin' ya. Have I ever kidded you guys? Ask Cool: Cool, am I tellin' the truth?"

"You tellin' the truth, man."

WILLIE

"Okay. Now, who knows what the Polo Grounds was?"

SECOND BOY

"That's where the Giants used to play before they moved to San Francisco."

"Right! And we're standin' right where it used to be. Home plate was right about here, where this manhole cover is." He taps it. "And the centerfield bleachers were four hundred eighty-five feet away. You know how far that is?" They shake their heads.

Willie points with his stick. "See that taxi?" He points to a cab parked three blocks away. "Well, right about there was the bleachers. Mule hit one in there. Didn't you, Mule?"

"Well, the wind was blowin' out."

Willie backs up a few paces and tosses Mule the stick. "Here, Mule, show 'em I'm not jivin'. <u>Kick it!</u>"

Willie pitches, Mule swings, the stick splinters into a hundred pieces, and the ball flies away. It comes down in front of the cab, bounces over it, and rolls into a sewer drain. The boys gape. Then they all begin talking at once and crowding around Mule.

BOYS

"How'd you do that, man?"

Mule hands another stick to the littlest boy. "Now you gotta get your feet in a good comfortable position... Not too close to the plate.... Now get that front shoulder around a little more...."

The camera pulls away as a circle of boys surrounds Mule in the middle of the street.

HALL OF FAME
Sandy Koufax has just finished speaking, and returns to his seat to loud applause.

"Thank you, Sandy ... Next, William "Willie" Mayberry!"

Willie, now graying in the temples and showing a bit of a paunch, stands and waves as the crowd erupts in cheers. He strides to the mike.

COMMISSIONER
(Reading from plaque:) "Second man to hit over six hundred home runs in major leagues... A great curve-ball hitter with a three-oh-five lifetime average... One of the finest outfielders the game has ever known. The man who made the basket catch famous."

Renewed whistles and cheers as Willie steps to the mike.

WILLIE
"I just want to say that I got a lot of help along the way. Especially when I was just a young kid, getting my first real coaching in the Negro Leagues.

"Without some of the men sitting here today, I never would have made it to the major leagues. You were like

fathers to me. I was still in high school when I started playing ball with the pro's I had twenty coaches. And also twenty baby sitters. Every night I'd hear a knock on my hotel room door: 'You all right in there?... Everything cool?' Every fifteen minutes! I didn't have a <u>chance</u> to get in trouble!"

Laughter.

"Artie Wilson was the last four hundred hitter in our leagues. He made it to the Giants, but he was a little too old, and when they signed me, they had to he him go. I always felt bad about that. Stand up, Artie."

"I just want to say to all you old-timers: You taught me to survive. You were the pioneers. You made it possible for all of us who came behind you."

Whistles and cheering. Willie waves and returns to his seat, stopping to embrace Cool and Mule.

COMMISSIONER

"James 'Cool' Bell!"

Cool, now bald, in a sports jacket with multi-colored jagged diagonal lines, gives his wheelchair wheels a spin, and sails across the stage, stopping on a dime. He does a fast one-quarter turn next to the Commissioner. A cheer goes up, and Cool replies with an enthusiastic wave.

COMMISSIONER

(Reading:) "One of fastest men ever to play the game... Could score from first on a fly ball... Or a sacrifice bunt... Batted three-ninety-two against white major leaguers."

He hands the mike to Cool, who looks around slowly.

"So this is the Hall of Fame? When I think of all the history I've seen. You know, I'm older than the airplane. I'm even older than Satchel." Cool turns and winks at Satch, who is seated behind him.

"In fact, I'm the only man that knows how old Satchel really is. He's one hundred and two. Because he's three years younger than me, and I'm a hundred and five."

Laughter.

"Those were a lot of great players back then. Now you take Mule Samson. Man, he set home run records in every park we played in. Did you know? He even stole my girl away from me."

In the audience Clara gasps in surprise and blows a kiss.

"But it never came between us in all those years.

"And talk about pitching! If Satch had been in the big leagues, he would have shaved some points off those high batting averages. And Smoky Joe Williams and Bullet Joe Rogan and Big Bill Foster would have shaved some more. Nobody has hit four hundred since our boys came into the league. Maybe that's not a coincidence.

"You know, we played most of the white stars, and I think we won a few more than we lost. Ain't that right, Satch?"

SATCHEL

"If you want to know the truth, wasn't any mebbe so."

COOL

"We were great players then. And we were cheated. This is America, and that never should have happened.

"And you were cheated too. Because most of you never got to see us play. You missed some of the greatest players ever played the game – Satchel, Dick Lundy, Biz Mackey – they say he was the best catcher of all-time, black or white – Ray Brown, Willie Wells. There were so many of 'em – they would have changed the record books. Josh or Mule, either one, would have broke Babe Ruth's record.

"And Oscar Charleston – they said he was the best Negro outfielder – John McGraw of the New York Giants said the best outfielder, period. Mister McGraw said he'd pay fifty thousand dollars for him if he was white. The only man could hit and run and throw with him was Willie Mayberry. You could put Willie and Charleston in a bag, and whichever one you pulled out, you couldn't go wrong."

Shouts from the audience: "What about you, Cool?"

"Well, they had it over me in hittin' homers, but I'd like to see if I could beat them in a race."

DOUBLE DUTY

(Shouts): "You could beat a horse!"

COOL

"This is the first time I've ever been here. We heard about the Hall of Fame. But we never thought it was <u>our</u> Hall of Fame. That was as foreign to us as a man walkin' on the moon. We never thought we would ever see such a day.

"They say we were born too soon. No. We weren't born too soon - they opened the doors too late."

Buck, Duty, and the others join in the applause as Cool gives the wheels a spin, and zips backs without looking, neatly to his place with the Mickey Mantle, Whitey 'Ford, and the other Hall of Famers.

COMMISSIONER

"George 'Mule' Samson."

Mule, balding and wearing glasses, rises unsteadily, leaning on a cane, and shuffles to the dais. Applause. Cameras flash. Clara blows a kiss, her eyes brimming with tears.

COMMISSIONER

"One of greatest sluggers the game has known... Led Negro League in home runs eight years.... Hit ten homers in only ninety-five at bats against barnstorming white big leaguers."

MULE

(Fumbling for words:) I'm not much good at talkin'..." He pulls a paper from his pocket and reads.

"First, I want to say thanks to the greatest hitter ever lived. Some say it was me, but this guy was the best I ever saw, and I've seen a lot of 'em, black and white. He should be standin' here instead of me: My brother, Charlie. Stand up, Charlie!"

The camera pans the guest section. At last a crutch rises from the seats, pointing up, and Charlie struggles to his feet and waves to applause.

"And I want to say thanks to my wife, Clara, I gave her a lot of bad times, and she always stuck by me. Without her, I wouldn't have made it. Thank you, Honey."

Clara's eyes tear up. She blows kisses.

"And I wish Mister Wilkinson was here today. He kept us goin' when times were rough. He slept with us and ate with us and mortgaged his house to make sure we got paid the first of every month.... Without him, I wouldn't be here. Jackie Robinson wouldn't be here..."

The players in the audience murmur, "You're right, brother."

Mule is no longer reading but is slowly warming to his subject.

"And my boy, Bobby Fielder. He always said I'd be here some day. I didn't believe him. But he was right."

Mule turns and bows slightly. Bobby smiles, makes a fist, and gives him a mock punch.

"There was a lot people helped us. Old guys like Candy Jim Taylor, Jud Wilson, Buck Leonard, Piper

Davis, Pop Lloyd, Bullet Rogan. I can't name 'em all."

The camera pans the faces of the old-timers on the lawn.

"... Double Duty Radcliffe - a million gals." Duty stands and takes several bows from the waist.

"Skinny Barnhill - a million laughs. Stood about this high" [he draws a line across his chest] "but the best spitball thrower in history."
                    SKINNY
"Naw, I never threw a spitter in my life." The players guffaw.

Just kiddin', Skinny. He didn't need no spitter. One time he relieved Satchel, threw nine pitches and struck 'em all out. They said, "You all done cut the legs off Satchel and sent him back out there!"

Buck and Duty playfully trade punches with Skinny.

"Buck Leonard - could sing like an angel and hit like the devil... Martin Dihigo -played anywhere in the field like he played there all his life...

Doc Sykes - he's the man saved eight innocent black kids from a lynchin'. Saved me too. Where you at, Doc? Stand up." Doc, 90, still tall and erect, slowly gets to his feet with the help of a cane, and waves. The gathering applauds.
                    PLAYERS
"You forgot Satchel!"
"Who?... Satchel who?"
                    SATCHEL
"You never could hit my "trouble ball."

"Well, maybe you did get me a few times. But I got you a few times too." He flashes a gleaming smile.

Someone on the lawn shouts: "What about Josh?"

MULE

"Yeah, we was always fightin' to be number-one. But he did something I never saw anybody do. We was playin' down in West Virginia, and he hit one over the fence, the second hit the bottom of a mountain. The next one went half-way up the mountain. And the last one went over the mountain!"

COOL

"That's right! I was there!"

MULE

"He would probably have gone to the Indians with you, Satch, if he hadn't died young."

SATCHEL

"If you want to know the truth, wasn't any mebbe so."

BUCK

"You forgot Louis Santop."

MULE

"Oh yeah. He was before my time. They say he hit one five hundred feet - and that was in the old dead ball days before Babe Ruth."

SATCHEL

"Don't forget Jose Mendez down in Cuba!"

MULE

"You're right. Threw a no-hitter against the Detroit Tigers back in nineteen oh-eight."

SATCHEL

"What about Cepeda?"

"Yeah, he's pretty good."

"No, not Orlando. I mean his daddy, Perucho."

"Yeah! Better than his son. Best hitter ever came out of Porta Rica."

Mule pauses. "They say, 'Too bad you never played against the best players.' But who's to say we didn't? I played against Satchel. I played against

Josh. I played against Dizzy. I played against Feller.

"Bullet Joe Rogan - a little bitty guy, but, man, could he hit 'em over the fence! And pitch! His curve ball looked like it dropped off a table. Could win twenty games and hit four hundred.

"And Smoky Joe Williams - what a fastball. He struck out about twenty New York Giants in one game, and I think the Giants won the pennant that year."
SATCHEL
"I pitched against him two times. He beat me one, I beat him one."
MULE
"Or you take Turkey Stearnes - as skinny as Ted Williams when Ted came up, and he could whip that ball just as far as Ted."

Turkey raises his hat.

"Hilton Smith - he used to relieve Satchel, and I don't know which one was harder to hit.

"How 'bout some of them <u>real</u> old timers, like Rube Foster, and Sol White [left]?"

"Willie Wells - what a shortstop! He would have made them forget all about Phil Rizzuto and Pee Wee Reese - he hit fifty points better than they did. And there wasn't a sign he couldn't steal!

"They all oughta be in the Hall of Fame."

"And Ted Williams. He's the one said, 'Open the doors, let these black boys in the Hall of Fame.'" Mule turns and nods to Ted, who gives him a two-finger salute and takes a playful swing of a bat.

TED

"Nobody in <u>our</u> league hit 'em any harder than <u>you</u> did, Mule."

"Mister Bob Feller. We went barnstormin' with him in 'forty-six. Coast-to-coast, first-class planes all the way. He had all the best players in the American League. We showed the fans some damn good baseball, and we all made good money, didn't we, Bob?"

Feller playfully winds up and "throws" a pitch toward Mule. "I'm glad I didn't have to pitch to you in the American League, Mule."

MULE

"Today I'm thankin' all those who helped us. And forgivin' all those who didn't.

"They say, 'Too bad you were born twenty years too soon.' Yeah, I wish we made some of this big money. But I say we were born right on time. We had a chance to do something for the Negro race.

"They say Jackie paved the way. He didn't pave the way.

"We did."

Mule stops, puts down his unused notes, looks lost for a moment, and shuffles to his seat. He stumbles, and Willie leaps up to steady him.

There's silence. Then a clap is heard, and another, then more. One by one the audience stands, the Hall of Famers stand, the black veterans and their wives stand, tears glistening on their cheeks.

The men on the dais converge on Mule and shake his hand. Then Mule and Cool file off the stage to greet their old friends and exchange hugs and slaps. Willie and Bobby join them and embrace old teammates to cries of "Bobby!".... "Duty!".... "Cool!"

Mule's kids have left the lawn and are swarming around him.

A fan with a camera asks everyone to pose, and they line up with friends and families, the boys kneeling in front.

The sepia photo of the Monarchs on the prairie is slowly super-imposed on the scene, gradually replacing it.

THE END

The world's top authority on the other half of baseball history, America's Negro Leagues, John B Holway interviewed over 70 veterans of that colorful era and compiled the most complete statistics ever done.

He has written 18 books, and has appeared in the *New York Times,* Washington *Post, Sports Illustrated,* and *USA Today,* plus CNN, ABC-TV, the History Channel, and magazines and newspapers from Boston to Los Angeles, Miami to Seattle, Tokyo to London, and Moscow to New Delhi.

A parachute lieutenant wounded in Korea, Holway has studied French, Japanese, Chinese, and Nepali. He picked up the last trekking around Annapurna in search of any black baseball vets who may have retired there.

Books

***Voices From the Great Black Leagues
**Complete Book of the Negro Leagues
Smoky Joe and the Cannonball
The Pitcher (with John Thorn)
Bullet Joe and the Monarchs
****Red Tails, Black Wings
Black Diamonds
Blackball Stars
Blackball Tales
Josh and Satch
Bloody Ground
Josh Gibson
*Sumo
Kick, Mule
The Sluggers
TED, The Kid
TED, The Man
TED, The Legend
Amazin' Baseball
The Last .400 Hitter
*Japan Is Big League in Thrills
Rube Foster, Father of Black Baseball

****Basis for the George Lucas film
***Casey Award, best baseball book, 1989
**SABR Bob Davids Award, 1986
*First books in English on the subject